THE RANSOM COMMANDO

Suave, ruthless and clever, Lorrimar is a man to reckon with. When he and his very professional underworld associates plan a heist, they mean it to be the last job of their criminal careers—the 'big one' which will set them up for life. In their well-planned operation of holding a millionaire businessman and his family to ransom, there is only one flaw. Unknown to them their captives secretly expect a very special guest... But there is barely time to recover from the shock of recognition before his unforeseen presence unleashes a terrifying chain of events. Captors and captives alike become the unwitting pawns in the kidnap plans of a terrorist group led by the callous Okada Kurusu.

THE RANSOM COMMANDO

James Grant

A Lythway Book

CHIVERS PRESS
BATH

First published in Great Britain 1978
by
Frederick Muller Limited
This Large Print edition published by
Chivers Press
by arrangement with Frederick Muller Limited
1983

ISBN 0 85119 981 X

British Library Cataloguing in Publication Data

Grant, James
    The ransom commando.—Large print ed.—(A
Lythway book)
    Rn: Bruce Crowther   I. Title
    823'.914[F]   PR6053.R657

    ISBN 0–85119–981–X

The author would like to thank Frank Watson for his invaluable assistance in the preparation of this book.

THE RANSOM COMMANDO

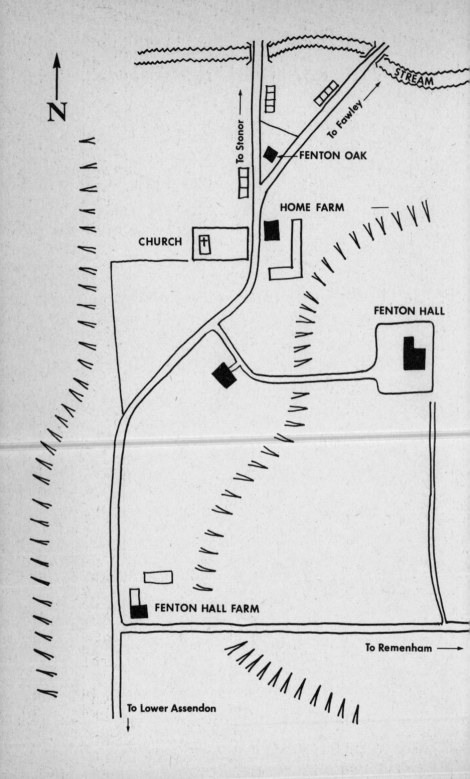

CHAPTER ONE

Lorrimar reached out and picked up his watch from the bedside table. As he fastened the strap he noted the time and then carefully easing his legs out of the bed, he stood up. The woman on the bed stirred briefly and then lay still again. He crossed to the window and pulled back the curtain. He could just make out the shape of the big house on the top of the hill, its outline uncertain against the backdrop of trees. There were a few lights on at the house and as he watched more were switched on. He shivered suddenly and moved back to the bed to pull on his trousers and a thin sweater. Back at the window he leaned into the bay and looked to his right, up the road that led to the church. After a few moments he saw the lights of a car cutting into the late afternoon dusk. He glanced at his watch again and then looked up in time to see the car turn to its right and disappear momentarily behind the darkening shape of Home Farm house. Then the lights of the car reappeared and moved slowly up the rise to the big house. It stopped, facing towards the village and Lorrimar involuntarily moved back into the room, almost as if there was a possibility that the driver would be able to see him. Then the car's headlights were switched off. He looked at his watch again. Four-thirty precisely.

'Like bloody clockwork,' he said quietly to himself. He pulled back the sheets and slapped the woman's thigh. The slap wasn't particularly gentle. She opened her eyes and looked at him. 'Get up,' he said. 'Time we were moving.' She sat up and Lorrimar stared openly at her heavy breasts. Give her a few more years, he thought, and she'll have no more shape than an all-in wrestler. He shrugged away the thought, he wouldn't know her then, so it would be something for someone else to worry about.

'What time is it?' she asked him.

'I've told you,' he said irritably. 'Time we were on our way.' The young woman hesitated, as if weighing the desirability of an assertive reply against the possibility that Lorrimar would react violently. She decided in favour of discretion and sulkily climbed out of the bed and walked across the room to where her clothes lay in a tumbled heap, contenting herself with a flaunting display of her body. Lorrimar watched her for a moment and then, as her actions began to arouse him, he moved quickly across the room, seized one of her heavy breasts in his right hand and pressed his weight against her so that she fell back across the bed. As she did so, she brought her face up to his, a small but triumphant smile showing briefly. Simultaneously she opened her legs wide and as Lorrimar felt the movement he ran his left hand down her body until it brushed roughly against her pubic hair. He bent his fingers and pushed them up into her, grinning tightly at her sudden gasp of pain.

'You should've learned that lesson by now,' he said. 'You don't do as you want, you do as I tell you.' He withdrew his hand and straightened up. He slipped off the thin sweater and then his trousers. The young woman looked at his face, hard and unsmiling and then her eyes moved down his body and, even after the few days they had spent together in the hotel room, she still felt the strange combination of alarm and excitement.

'Hell Dave,' she said. 'You're a big bastard.' He didn't speak as he knelt on the bed. This time she was ready for him and they began to move rhythmically together, his weight spread on either side of her so that all she could feel was that part of him that was inside her.

She tried to hold herself back but she couldn't and as she shuddered and arched her back, forcing herself against him, he eased backwards and out of her. She tried to hold him to her.

'That's another lesson you should've learned,' he said and rolled over onto his back. She twisted round on the bed and brought her mouth down onto his erection and for the first time she felt some control over him and as he came she marked it as a victory. It wasn't a victory that lasted long. Lorrimar pushed her off him and stood up.

'Right,' he said. 'Get moving, I want to be out of here in ten minutes.' He began to dress, his movements neat and efficient. Then he packed his remaining clothes into the soft leather Gucci grip that lay on the stand at the foot of the bed.

'I'll be downstairs,' he told her. He picked up the grip and went out of the room closing the door behind him without noise. The woman looked at the closed door, mouthed a silent obscenity and then hurriedly continued her own packing. She knew better than to keep him waiting.

At the foot of the stairs Lorrimar paused and listened, he heard a sound of someone whistling in the bar and he pushed open the door and walked in. There was only one man in the room, and he looked up as Lorrimar came in. Simon Arne had owned the Fenton Oak for ten years and in that time he had learned to assess people swiftly and, usually, accurately. He didn't like the heavy-set, dark haired man who now dropped the expensive-looking suitcase on the floor and reached into his pocket for his wallet. But he had also learned to conceal his dislikes from his customers and he switched on his best smile.

'Ready for the off?' he asked.

'Yes,' Lorrimar said, nodding.

'I'll get your bill,' Arne said and turned to go through into the small office behind the bar.

'Don't bother,' Lorrimar said. He threw some notes onto the bar. 'No point in letting the tax man have his share is there. That'll cover it.' He grinned slightly, his teeth shining whitely beneath his heavy, drooping moustache. Arne shrugged his shoulders, the gesture the other man had made seemed somehow to annoy him.

'Thank you sir,' he said and picked up the money. He glanced at it. 'There is too much here,' he said.

'That's alright,' Lorrimar said. 'Worth it.' He turned away and picked up the grip. 'Be seeing you.' He walked out of the bar and Arne heard his footsteps fade down the hall towards the door that opened into the car park. A moment later he heard the woman's footsteps on the stairs and he went through into the hallway. She was struggling down with a suitcase, a handbag and a heavy, full-length suede coat over her arm. He reached up and took the case from her.

'You should have called,' he told her reprovingly. 'Too much for a lady to manage on her own.' The woman smiled at him. The smile seemed to tell him that gentlemen were not her customary associates. He carried the case out into the car park where Lorrimar was sitting in a pale blue Daimler Sovereign, the boot lid standing open. Arne put the case in the boot and closed it. The woman was already climbing into the front passenger seat and he moved round and closed the door. He waved at the woman as

5

the car moved slowly out of the car park and turned left into the lane. He went back into the inn and walked up the stairs and into the room the couple had occupied. He glanced around and then checked through the drawers and cupboards. They had left nothing behind and he hadn't really expected them to have done so. The man, Lorrimar, if that was his real name, hadn't looked like the kind of man who left things behind in hotel rooms. Arne opened the window and went back down the stairs and into the bar. Friday nights were busy at the Oak and it wouldn't do to be unprepared for the fray.

At the junction with the main road Lorrimar paused, the traffic was light and he hadn't long to wait before there was a gap big enough for the Daimler to slip into. He didn't speak until they were through Henley-on-Thames and heading for Maidenhead and the M4 spur.

'I'll drop you at the club,' he told the woman.

'Will you be in later Dave?' she asked.

'Doubt it.'

'Oh, what about tomorrow night?'

'Expect so. About ten.' The woman nodded and leaned towards him. She placed a tentative hand on his thigh.

'Thanks Dave,' she said. 'I enjoyed it. Nice to get out into the country. Pity it isn't summer though.' Lorrimar didn't answer and the woman moved her hand slowly higher.

'Not when I'm driving,' he said sharply and

she snatched away her hand.

'Sorry Dave,' she said. She moved away from him and looked out of the window into the darkness. It would have been an exaggeration to have said she was afraid of him. She wasn't, but he made her uneasy, unable to relax. She sensed that if she said or did anything that went too far there would be trouble. Trouble that would end with her getting hurt. So far he hadn't hurt her but she had been extra careful with him. If talk was anything to go by then he could be nasty when things went wrong.

It was raining steadily when they reached London and Lorrimar stopped the car in Old Compton Street and climbed out to unlock the boot. He lifted out the woman's case and turned to climb back in.

'I'll see you tomorrow then Dave,' she said. He paused and turned back. The woman stepped towards him and held up her face to be kissed but Lorrimar ignored her and reached into his pocket.

'Here,' he said and pushed something into her hand. He climbed back into the Daimler and started the engine. He drove away leaving her standing on the pavement. She opened her hand and looked at the notes he had given her. Part of her felt that she would have preferred him to have kissed her, or to have at least said something pleasant. Then her materialism recognised that his generosity with money more

7

than made up for his lack of emotion. She pushed the money into her handbag and picked up the suitcase. She walked the short distance to the club and went in through the front door. The flat-eyed man at the door watched her as she walked in. He held out his hand and she stopped and stood the case on the floor. She took out the money Lorrimar had given her and handed it to the man. He counted it out into two piles and handed the smaller pile back to her.

'He must have worked you hard,' he said. She ignored him and picked up her case and went on up the stairs in silence.

Lorrimar parked the car in Montpelier Place and walked through a passageway into a mews. The wet cobblestones were shining in the light of the street lamps and he turned up his collar as the wind gusted the rain into his face. He stopped outside the white-painted door of one of the mews cottages. He rang the bell and waited. When the door opened he went in.

Inside, the cottage was a superb example of the combination of unlimited money and severely limited taste. There were few signs left of the original tasteful decor and the additions, since the last owner had moved out, were slowly taking over. If Lorrimar noticed he gave no sign. He didn't like the place, not for its interior design but because it was one of the very few places he went where he wasn't the top man. He took off his overcoat and handed it to the old

8

man who had opened the door. He went through into the dining room. The others were already there, sitting at the big table. He sat down and nodded at the man at the head of the table. Kenneth Mannion was the same age as Lorrimar, forty-five, but there was nothing in their appearance that showed any similarity. Mannion was three inches shorter than Lorrimar's five feet ten, he was fat and looked unfit against Lorrimar's heavily muscled, hard body. His hair was as dark as Lorrimar's but there was very little of it left and what there was had been carefully dressed to conceal a rapidly expanding bald patch. Only their eyes were similar, dark and unusually expressionless. The two other men were very different. James Hart was thirty-eight and looked younger. He was the same height as Lorrimar but his thinness made him appear taller. His hair was very blond and wispy and his eyes were a bright blue that bored into anyone he looked at, but usually he didn't look at people, tending to efface himself whenever possible. Unlike Mannion who was wearing an expensive cashmere sweater and a pair of casual trousers, well-tailored to hide his protruding stomach, Hart wore a shabby but gaudy jacket made up of small pieces of different coloured suede. He had on a pale blue cheesecloth shirt and around his neck was a necklace of bright green wooden beads. Lorrimar looked at him and wondered why he didn't find Hart distasteful. He was used to seeing homosexuals around and at times they had their uses, particularly when a little leverage was needed on some of the clients at the various clubs they operated, but usually he avoided their company. Hart was different. Apart from his slightly outlandish mode of dress he rarely said or did anything that indicated where his sexual proclivities lay. His speech was quite normal with none of the camp words or phraseology that many of his show-business friends used. Lorrimar decided that it was Hart's reputation that made him see him with less critical eyes. Although he had never been on a job with him he knew of his extraordinary, almost legendary ability with weapons. Hart was known as the best mechanic in the country. He had been asked to take his talents elsewhere which suggested that he was one of the best in the world. But he hadn't taken up any of the offers. He claimed he didn't want to leave London and that, Lorrimar felt, was the only disturbing thing about him. The other man at the table was small, about five feet six. His smallness, sandy hair and pale blue eyes made his age hard to determine but he was around forty. Quick in his movements and filled with nervous energy he seemed an unlikely man to use on a difficult operation but Lorrimar had worked with him before and he knew that once on a job the little man's nervousness disappeared, channelled into an aggressive dynamism that had, in the past, pulled him out of many tight corners. Lorrimar nodded at the little man.

'Hello Bill. How's Mum?' Bill McKendrick looked at the bigger man.

'She's alright Dave. Sends her love.'

'I'll bet. What did she really say?'

'Unrepeatable,' the little man said. He glanced sideways at Hart. 'Especially in mixed company.' The thin, fair-haired man looked at McKendrick.

'How would you like it if I put a little calling card in your bathroom?' he asked amiably. The others grinned. One of Hart's better-known gestures had been to rig the lavatory of someone who had offended him, with a minute charge of plastic explosive. The charge had been wired to explode when a pressure switch under the seat had been operated. As the story went, the pressure switch had been set to operate only when a certain weight was applied, the offending person being somewhat overweight. How much of it was true no one knew. What was certain, however, was that the man concerned lived to tell the tale but no longer had any cause to comment on Hart's sexuality—or anyone else's for that matter. Mannion cleared his throat.

'Okay, let's begin,' he said. The others pulled their chairs closer to the table.

11

'Who else is here?' Lorrimar asked.

'Just old Sid. He's through in the back and can't hear. Anyway he's okay.'

'Who else is coming?'

'Nobody. We're all here.' Lorrimar looked at Mannion, surprise showing clearly in his face.

'Three of us? That's not on, Ken. It will be tight with four, but three isn't on at all.'

'There are four. I'm coming in as the fourth man.' Lorrimar looked at Mannion, his eyes screwing up as he considered the other man's words. He glanced at the others. McKendrick's face didn't convey anything. It was likely that he didn't much care. One of his best qualities was his unquestioning allegience to the team he was working with and his ability to take orders, any orders and act on them without hesitation. The expression in Hart's eyes showed clearly that his mind was working the same way as Lorrimar's. Lorrimar turned back to Mannion.

'I think you'd better explain,' he said. Mannion's lips tightened and for a moment there was tension in the room. Then he grinned and the tension eased.

'Yes, okay, I expect you're right Dave. It's a long time since I've been on a job. You know me best as the man with the ideas and the money to set up the operations. That doesn't mean I don't know how to do the work myself. I did a bit in the old days.'

'I know you did. But it *was* a bit, you never

ran a team. And it *was* in the old days. Things are different now and this job isn't a place for an amateur.'

'Amateur.' Mannion spat out the word and the tension came back. 'Cut it out Dave. I'm no amateur and you know it.' He waved his arm at the room. 'I didn't get all this, or the place in Portugal, or the boat by being a bloody amateur.'

'You're not an amateur at what you do Ken,' Lorrimar said calmly. 'You get the ideas, you set up the jobs, you plan them and you pick the right teams. As far as I can remember you've never had a bad deal. The few that failed did so because of factors outside your control. That makes you a professional at doing your job. It doesn't make you a professional at doing our job.'

'Okay Dave. I know what you're saying is right but there's a reason.'

'What?'

'You agree that four is the right number.'

'Five or even six would be the right number. Four is the minimum and it's near the mark.'

'Maybe. What you can't argue about is that there aren't another three like you three around. So we couldn't have made it six. As for five, well we might have made that number up, but Charlie got himself nicked three months ago and that only leaves Eddie.'

'What's wrong with Eddie?' Mannion looked

13

across the table at Lorrimar.

'Simple arithmetic, that's what's wrong.' He paused for a moment. 'Work it out for yourself Dave. All of you. With Eddie in that makes four on the job and me. That's five. If I take Eddie's place then there are only four. Divide the take by four and you get a bigger answer than if you divide by five.'

'And if there's a cock-up there won't be any take to divide by anything.'

'There won't be a cock-up. Look, what would Eddie have done that I can't?'

'You're out of practice.'

'You know I can do it.'

'No.'

'Then we call it off.' Mannion pushed back his chair and stood up. The others looked at him and then at each other. Hart leaned back in his chair and smiled humourlessly at Lorrimar.

'Wait a minute Dave,' he said. He looked up at Mannion. 'Dave would still be in charge of the operation?'

'Of course he would. Christ, Dave, there isn't any suggestion that I take over from you. You still run the show and I take orders from you once we're out there. It wouldn't work any other way.' There seemed no doubt that he was sincere, but still Lorrimar hesitated.

'It means you'll have to leave the country when it's over. Like the rest of us.'

'I know that.'

14

'I never thought you wanted to leave. I thought you liked it here.' Mannion sat down again.

'I was at the villa last month,' he said. 'I go there for about six weeks every year, that's all. It's big and it's less than fifty yards from the sea. The sun shines all the time and the food's good and . . . Christ what does anyone want to stop here for?' Lorrimar nodded slowly. He didn't believe the other man but there wasn't anything he could hang his feelings on. He thought for a moment longer. There didn't seem to be too many things that Mannion could do on the job that would cause problems. Not if he did as he had said he would and took orders. He glanced at Hart and tried to read his thoughts.

'Okay,' he said eventually. 'We do it with the four of us. Remember though, if I say we abort, then we abort. No arguments.' Mannion nodded, his relief showing in his broad smile.

'Of course Dave.' He stood up again and walked across to the small circular bar that stood against one wall of the room. He brought four glasses and an ice bowl back to the table. 'Usual?' he asked. The others nodded their heads. Lorrimar looked at Hart as Mannion turned away and this time there was no doubt about Hart's feelings. He didn't like the inclusion of Mannion in the operational team any more than Lorrimar did. By unspoken consent the two men agreed to meet later. It was

15

necessary for them to talk. Mannion came back to the table with a bottle of scotch and a bottle of vodka. He stood the vodka in front of Hart and poured scotch into the other three glasses. Hart poured his own drink and then Mannion sat down and took charge of the meeting once more.

'Okay Dave. Let's have your report.' Lorrimar sipped at his drink and waited until he had the full attention of the others.

'Okay,' he said. 'Ken's seen the place...'

'Only a glimpse,' the fat man interrupted. 'I drove through the village but I didn't stop.' Lorrimar nodded and took a sheet of paper from his pocket and spread it on the table. The others leaned forward.

'Yeah, okay. Well, the road into the village off the main road starts just outside Lower Assendon, it's called Fenton Lane. It's a straight road for about half a mile. A third of the way along the straight there's a right turn, Remenham Lane, leading to Remenham village. There's a farmhouse on the corner. Big place with a lot of outbuildings. It's called Fenton Hall Farm. About three hundred yards down Remenham Lane there's a footpath leading off to the left. It goes along the edge of a field and comes out at the south-east corner of Fenton Hall. That's the back way in, your way Bill. If you pass the Remenham Lane end, about six hundred yards further on along Fenton Lane,

16

the road bends to the right, a couple of hundred yards after the bend there is a turning on the right. That's the main drive up to the Hall. Half way up the hill to the Hall there's a cottage off to the right. The servants live there.'

'Servants, bloody hell,' McKendrick muttered.

'He looks after the gardens and she's the housekeeper,' Lorrimar went on. He glanced at Mannion questioningly. 'You reckoned they wouldn't be a problem?'

'That's right. I'll explain later. Carry on Dave.'

'Okay. Just past where the drive goes up to the Hall there's a left hand bend and the road passes between a farm on the right and the church on the left. The farm, it's called Home Farm, stands close to the road side. The church is well back from the road. The graveyard is in front of it. Just past the graveyard there's a row of what used to be three cottages. Now, the first one is a shop. The people who own it live above and next door. Right outside, the road forks. Straight on, it goes up to Stonor; to the right it leads to Fawley. In the middle of the fork is the pub. The car park is at the rear and leads out into Stonor Lane. Just past the car park entrance on the same side of the road are four cottages. On the Fawley road there are four more cottages on the left at the back of the car park. That's it for buildings. Just beyond the

17

houses on Stonor Lane and on Fawley Road there are hump-back bridges over a stream. It's the same stream that runs west to east.' Lorrimar picked up his drink and sipped at it again. 'Now for the people. No problems that I can see. All what you would expect. The guy that owns the pub is one of those clever, ex-army, colonel types. Thinks the world would be put right if they brought back hanging and flogging. The local copper lives in the next village and comes through twice a day. About eight-thirty in the morning and again at just before closing time. He calls in the pub, has a drink and then clears off before he's in danger of catching them doing any after hours drinking. The people in the cottages mostly work on the farms in the district although a couple of the cottages have been bought and tarted up by people from outside. Nobody I saw will give us any problems even if we see them, which isn't very likely. The two farms I mentioned both have fields that adjoin the grounds of the Hall and both the farmers go for a walk round each night before they go to bed. Still no problems because at this time of year their sheep are close in to the farms while they're lambing and the fields near the hall are empty. Now for the target. Ken will give us the layout of the Hall. I haven't been inside it, of course. I haven't even been up to it. As for the people, they do everything to the book. Garroway is as regular

18

as clockwork. Goes out at seven-thirty on the dot. Gets back four-thirty. The three days I was there he was within half a minute every time. Our other reports say the same. His wife stays at home every morning. In the afternoons she goes out. I didn't follow her but we know she goes into Maidenhead one day to see her Mother, three days she does social work at one of the hospitals in Reading and on one day she comes up here to London.'

'Weekends?' Hart asked. Lorrimar looked at Mannion.

'That's part of your information,' he said. Mannion nodded and reached out for the bottle and refilled his and the other whisky drinker's glasses.

'That's right,' he said. 'Garroway works a five day week, every weekend in the winter he spends at home. Rarely goes out, rarely has visitors. His wife generally stays with him, occasionally visits friends. The older daughter works in London and lives here through the week. Most weekends she goes home.'

'How do we know she'll be there the weekend we pick?' Hart asked.

'Because we'll pick a weekend when we know she'll be there.'

'How do we know that?' McKendrick asked. Mannion looked at him, a trace of irritation in his eyes, then he grinned.

'Go back to sleep Bill,' he said. 'That's what I

19

get paid for.' The small sandy-haired man nodded.

'Sorry Ken,' he said.

'What about friends?' Lorrimar asked. 'Doesn't she have any visitors?' Mannion hesitated and Lorrimar saw something in his eyes, something that he couldn't quite identify.

'Not often,' Mannion said, his eyes regaining their normal impassive look. 'If she does then I expect we can take care of it. The younger girl, she hasn't any friends in the village, so there are no problems of her having visitors.'

'No school friends?'

'She goes to a private school near Wantage. Lives in and goes home occasional weekends.'

'And I expect we're going in on a weekend we know she'll be at home,' Hart said. Mannion grinned.

'Right,' he said. He looked at the thin, fair haired man and his expression became thoughtful. 'Any mechanical problems?' he asked.

'No. Everything's okay,' Hart answered. 'We agreed we're using Dave's Daimler to go in. When we come out we can use either it or Garroway's Rolls or both.' He looked enquiringly at Lorrimar.

'With only four of us I'm not too happy at splitting into two groups. It weakens our hold,' Lorrimar said. He looked at Mannion. The plump man shook his head gently and Lorrimar shrugged. 'Okay we'll take the Rolls, seven of us will be a squeeze but there's always the possibility that we won't need to take Garroway. I'll decide later, when I know how he's reacting.' He looked at Hart. 'What about shooters?'

'Six,' Hart said. 'One each and two spares.'

'What have you got?' McKendrick asked.

'For Dave and me I've got .44 Smith & Wessons. I've got you your favourite Bill. A nine millimetre single-action Beretta.' He looked at Mannion. 'The others are a Walther PPK nine millimetre semi-automatic which I expected Eddie to have, a .32 Smith & Wesson and a Ceska .75 millimetre automatic. Take your pick.' Mannion hesitated before answering and then, sensing that his hesitation showed weakness, made up his mind in a hurry.

'I'll have the Smith & Wesson. Six shot is it?'

'No, it's one of the new ones, five shot. Won't spoil the shape of your suit.' Hart grinned slightly and Lorrimar looked away to avoid smiling. He knew Mannion's sensitivity over remarks about his wardrobe.

'Anything else?' Mannion asked.

'Yeah, two rifles.'

'Rifles?' Mannion sounded surprised and Lorrimar felt again the small nag of doubt.

'Yes, two AKM's. Useful if the law tries any long range aggro.'

'Yes, I expect we need them. That all?'

'I suppose we'll all have our own ideas about what to fill our pockets with,' Hart said quietly. Mannion looked irritably at the fair-haired man.

'I'd like to know,' he said. Lorrimar glanced at him.

'I thought we'd agreed the operation was my concern,' he said. Mannion's face darkened and then he nodded.

'Yes, sorry Dave.' He looked at Hart. 'That the lot?'

'Yes.'

'Right. The details of the operation should be clear to all of us by now but we'd better run through it again. Do you want to do it Dave or shall I?' Lorrimar shrugged his shoulders. Privately he knew the plan backwards and he was mildly irritated at Mannion's insistence at going over it every few days. He switched his mind to other things and let Mannion's voice float over him. Once during the following ten minutes he focussed his eyes on Hart and was immediately aware that, like him, the thin man was thinking about other things. When Mannion had finished Lorrimar eased back his chair and began to rise to his feet.

'What about disguises, masks or whatever we're going to use?' Mannion asked. Lorrimar looked at him.

'None,' he said.

'None?'

'No, why should we bother? We're getting

out of the country right afterwards and we're not coming back. Ever.'

'Yes, but, maybe it would be best if we did something. Just in case.'

'Look,' Lorrimar said, a trace of irritation creeping into his voice. 'It's all worked out, the way we're doing it. It means that everyone will know who we are and what we're doing. By the time we're ready to move out our faces will be all over the front page of every paper and on every television screen. Masks are a waste of time.'

'But . . .'

'No buts Ken. No masks and no false names.'

'Names?'

'Why not? I used my real name at the pub.'

'You did, Jesus Christ Dave, why?'

'I've already said it mate. Why not?'

'But what if somebody recognised you while you were there? Or recognised your name?'

'Who? The village copper? Anyway if he's smart enough to have recognised the name then he's smart enough to have recognised the face and if he did that and then found I was registered under a false name he would have had the big boys down from the Met. My way, if I was recognised, they would think I was just having a dirty weekend with a bird.'

'Couldn't have any other kind with Linda,' McKendrick remarked and Hart and Lorrimar laughed. Mannion did not join in but after a moment he nodded his head slowly.

'Okay Dave,' he said. 'We do it your way.'

They left Mannion's separately, McKendrick first, then Hart, then Lorrimar. Outside it had stopped raining and the air was bitterly cold. Frost had already begun to sparkle on the cobblestones in the mews as Lorrimar walked briskly to his car. As he unlocked the door he heard Hart's voice behind him.

'Time for a drink Dave?'

'Yes, get in Jim. I think we need to talk.'

'Agreed.' Hart slid his long legs into the car and stretched back in the seat. 'Are you thinking what I'm thinking?'

'If you're thinking that Ken's up to something then the answer is yes.'

'That's exactly what I'm thinking,' Hart said. Lorrimar started the engine and the Daimler moved forward softly into the thickening traffic heading for the West End.

'Where?' Lorrimar asked. 'The Bear or the Longboat?'

'Better make it somewhere private,' Hart said. 'What about Harry's?'

'Okay,' Lorrimar said.

*　　　*　　　*

In the mews cottage Mannion sat at the table staring into space. After a long time he stood up and opened the door and shouted down the hall. The old man who had taken Lorrimar's overcoat shuffled up from the kitchen.

'Tidy up Sid,' Mannion said. 'Usual.' The old man nodded and went into the dining room and began putting glasses on to a tray. Then he gathered up several pieces of paper including the map Lorrimar had brought. He went through into the kitchen and carefully washed the glasses. Then he put the papers into a metal waste bin and set light to them. When they had burned he ran water into the bin from the tap and poured the resulting black mess into the sink and left the tap running until everything had been washed from sight. Then he turned up the sound on his television set and sat down at the table where he had been sitting all evening.

In his bedroom Mannion had been waiting for the sound of the television set. When he heard it he pulled the telephone towards him and dialled. It was answered immediately.

'All set,' he said. He waited, listening. 'Right,' he said after a moment. 'Next Saturday it is.' He hung up the receiver and stretched out on the bed. His stomach churned angrily and he regretted the extra glass of whisky he had drunk. Not that it mattered all that much, he wasn't likely to get much sleep that night anyway.

CHAPTER TWO

It was twenty minutes before closing time when the police Landrover drew up outside the Fenton Oak. Although only twenty-seven, Police Constable Raymond Blake was both experienced and far-sighted. He knew which of the pubs in his area were potential trouble spots and those that were not. The Oak was quite definitely in the second category. Simon Arne had a nose for trouble-makers and they seldom got beyond a second drink. Blake grinned slightly to himself as he went in through the front door and down the hallway to the door that opened into the office behind the bar. If he had been a resident of Fenton he doubted very much that he would have been a regular at the Oak. He didn't dislike Arne, but he never felt quite at ease with him either. There was too much of the ex-army aura about the man. He had the feeling that he was always under inspection. He let himself into the office and sat on the edge of Arne's desk. The room was like Arne, neat, efficient and just a shade too masculine. He wondered what Arne's wife had been like. He knew that the villagers, who remembered her, thought highly of her and said that Arne had been a better man when she was still alive. He was lost in his thoughts when the second door to the office, the one that led into the area behind the bar, opened and Arne came in. He carried a glass containing Blake's nightly whisky and water. The policeman took the glass and handed Arne the price of the drink. The Oak was the only place where he took a drink and he always ensured it was paid for, that way there could never be any misunderstanding between them.

'All quiet Mr. Arne?' It was his usual question.

'All quiet Mr. Blake.' The answer too was usual and it had become part of their routine. Blake sipped his drink.

'I checked on your visitor,' he said after a moment.

'Lorrimar?'

'Yes, that really is his name.'

'I guessed wrong then.'

'Only about that. You were right when you said you thought he was a man to watch.'

'Oh? Who is he?'

'They know him very well at the Met. A big-time villain it seems.'

'What did he want here I wonder?'

'Did? He's gone then?'

'Yes, went this afternoon about five.'

'Oh. Well, he isn't wanted for anything and he made no attempt to conceal his identity, and he used his own car, that's how I found out who he was.'

'What about the woman? Was it his wife?'

'No, your instinct was right there as well. His wife's dead. Doesn't appear to have a regular woman, so she could have been almost anyone. Maybe that's why he was out here, a few days alone with her. Maybe she was married to somebody else.'

'No, I don't think she was married at all.'

'Anyway, if he's gone, that's it. The powers that be know about it and if there's any significance they'll find it. After all, there can't be anything out here for a big-time operator like Lorrimar.' Blake finished his drink and handed the glass back to Arne. 'Thanks a lot for telling me anyway. It all helps.'

'Promotion on its way?' Arne asked.

'I'm sitting a board next month. Fingers crossed.'

'I wish you luck but I'll be sorry to see you go. They will move you if you are made sergeant won't they?'

'It's usual.' The door to the bar opened and a slightly harrassed-looking man put his head into the room.

'Sorry, Mr. Arne, but it's getting a bit hectic out here.' Arne nodded.

'I'll be right there Peter,' he said. The policeman walked across to the other door.

'I'll be on my way then. Good night Mr. Arne.'

'Goodnight Mr. Blake,' Arne said. The policeman went out of the pub and climbed into the Landrover. He drove up the road towards the A423 glancing up the drive that led to the Hall as he passed the entrance. Must be nice to have money, he thought. Then he changed his mind. Apart from the Rolls-Royce and the big house, Sir James Garroway didn't seem to have a lot to show for his reputedly vast wealth.

*   *   *

That same evening found the Golden Ball considerably less crowded than the Fenton Oak. There were only five customers there when Lorrimar and James Hart walked in. Known to its habitués as Harry's, the pub was in a side street off New Bond Street and had a massive lunch-time trade from shop and office workers, but in the evenings and at weekends, when the area was almost deserted, it was a good place to take another man's wife or to have a meeting you didn't want observed or overheard. Lorrimar let Hart buy the drinks and they took them into a corner of the room.

'Are we both thinking the same thing then Dave?' Hart asked.

'Probably. Ken is hiding something and I can't decide what.'

'That's the feeling I have. Let's talk and see if we come up with any ideas.'

'Okay,' Lorrimar said. 'First, there's the fact that he is coming in himself. He knows that it's a big operation and dangerous and that he's out of practice.' He paused and looked at Hart over the glass. 'That enough for starters?'

'Yeah. I had the same thoughts. There's more though.'

'Go on.'

'Apart from him being wrong for this job, Bill's wrong too. And for that matter I'm not even sure I'm right for it.'

'You're the best there is.'

'I know that, I didn't mean I was wrong in that way. I mean . . .' Hart's voice trailed off. Lorrimar leaned forward.

'You mean because you don't really want to leave the country?' Hart nodded slowly.

'Me and Bill. He won't go without his old Mum and it isn't likely she'll want to go.'

'Leave Bill for the moment. Why are you in if you don't want to leave the country?' Hart grinned at Lorrimar.

'Why? The money of course. No one has ever set up a paypacket like this one before. I don't want to go but I can't afford to turn down that kind of money.'

'And Bill?'

'I haven't asked him but I reckon that's the way his mind is working too.'

'It still leaves the old girl. He won't go without her and, as you said yourself, it isn't likely she'll go.' Hart drained his glass.

'Right,' he said. 'So that brings us back to

where we started. Why are we in the team? Not you, I don't suppose you care where you live for the rest of your life. But why did he pick me and Bill.'

'Because you're the right men for the job and . . .'

'And?'

'And maybe he isn't too worried about what happens afterwards.'

'A double cross? Would he dare?'

'Not on his own.'

'You mean he might have another team lined up to take care of us?'

'Doesn't seem likely does it?' Lorrimar said. 'We do the job, we share out the money. What advantage would he gain for bringing in another team to take us out? He would still have to share with them. Doesn't make sense. Maybe we're making something out of nothing.'

'Maybe. Still we'd better ask around. Quickly too. Could be any time now.'

'You're right,' Lorrimar said. 'It will be soon. Okay, I'll ask around. See if there are any likely candidates. You keep an eye on Mannion.' Lorrimar paused. 'Better not say anything to Bill.'

'Right.' Hart leaned back in his chair. 'Another drink?'

'No, not for me. You stopping?'

'No. Not enough life here. Can you drop me near the Longboat?'

'Sure.' The two men stood up and walked out of the pub. In the Daimler Lorrimar hesitated before starting the engine. 'Apart from the guns you told us about earlier, have you anything else you can lay your hands on quick?'

'Such as?'

'Anything. Just so long as it's something Mannion doesn't know about.' Hart grinned, his teeth gleaming in the darkness of the car's interior.

'You've been reading my mind Dave. Yeah, I've got a couple of things that might help to equalise matters if he is trying something on. I'll call round at your place tomorrow. Okay?' Lorrimar nodded his head.

'Good man. That will let me sleep easier.' He started the car and drove off towards Old Compton Street.

CHAPTER THREE

The report on Lorrimar's short stay at the Fenton Oak eventually found its way on to a desk at Scotland Yard's Serious Crimes office. It was read by a chief inspector who later made a telephone call. The man he spoke to called him back two days later. After the call the chief inspector rang down to the sergeant who had made out the report sheet.

'Don't think there's anything for us,' he told the sergeant. 'Lorrimar isn't doing anything he shouldn't be doing. His clubs are still making money out of the mugs and there are no whispers about any tickles in the offing. He was probably having a few days relaxation. Mind you he won't have had too much of that, not if what they tell me about the woman is right. She's Linda Hooper and she has hidden talents. I've added her name to the report. Pass a good word down to Thames Valley about the copper that sent in the report. Sharp-eyed lad.' He replaced the receiver and put the report in his out-tray.

*　　　*　　　*

About the same time that the Yard man was talking about him, Lorrimar was driving away from Mannion's mews cottage. He drove carefully and his tension was betrayed only by the set of his jaw. He crossed Hyde Park and parked the Daimler in Queensway and walked the rest of the way to the Hatherley Grove flat that Hart rented. He rang the bell and waited. Hart's voice grated from the grille beside the door. Lorrimar spoke into the grille and a moment later he heard a dull click as Hart released the lock. Lorrimar ran lightly up the stairs to the third floor. He was breathing normally when he got to Hart's door. The tall, thin man had opened the door and Lorrimar went straight in.

'Well?' Hart was standing expectantly in the middle of the room.

'This Saturday.'

'What time?'

'We go into the house at nine-fifteen.'

'What time do we start?'

'Six. I'll pick you up here. Then we pick up Bill at his Mum's and then Ken at the mews. That way your cars are all in your own garages.'

'Does it matter?'

'Not really but it's tidier that way.' Lorrimar looked speculatively at Hart. 'Mannion wanted me to pick him up first, but I didn't want him to see what you'll be putting in the boot.'

'Good thinking. We need our little surprise. Just in case.'

'You're sure you'll have all your personal loose ends tied up by Saturday?'

'Yes,' Hart answered. 'All that need doing, apart from one or two but none that will make the law look at me too carefully before then. After Saturday, well, it won't matter will it?'

'Right.' Lorrimar turned away. 'I'll go and see Bill. I know it's a bit late in the day, but it's time I found out what his Mum thinks about all this.'

McKendrick lived with his mother in a ground floor flat in a prison-like block of red-brick buildings in Barnes. Lorrimar parked the

34

Daimler and walked through the arched entrance into the inner courtyard and threaded his way through lines of washing hanging out to dry. He rang the bell on the door of number nine and waited. The door swung open after several moments and McKendrick looked at him with enquiry changing to surprise and alarm on his face.

'Dave. What are you...?' he paused, recovering himself. 'It's on is it? I thought you would ring.'

'Let me in then Bill. Can't talk out here can we?' Lorrimar said.

'Oh, yeah, sorry Dave. A bit of a surprise that's all. Come in.' He led the way down a narrow passage made still narrower by a clutter of miscellaneous household equipment. Lorrimar hadn't been to the flat for over a year and he had remembered it as a place where nothing was ever out of place and everywhere always sparkled as if just polished by a team of house-proud cleaners. He followed McKendrick into the small living room with its net-curtained windows looking out into the road where he had parked his car. The windows needed cleaning and the net curtains, supposedly white, were a grubby grey. He sat down, unasked, and looked up at McKendrick.

'Where's Mum?' he asked.

'Er, she's still in bed. Not feeling too good.' Lorrimar started to get up again.

'I'd better go in and see her,' he said.

'No.' McKendrick snapped the word. Lorrimar sank back into the chair.

'Time you told me what's going on Bill,' he said mildly.

'What do you mean?'

'Come on, you know what I mean. You'll never go to live abroad for the rest of your natural. Not without your Mum and she'll not leave England will she? Christ, it's a major operation getting her to leave London for a couple of days.' McKendrick nodded his head slowly and dropped into a chair opposite Lorrimar.

'Yes, okay Dave. You're right. Mum won't be going because she can't. She's dying. Cancer.' Lorrimar looked at the other man, his face reflecting his thoughts.

'Oh, bloody hell,' he said. 'Christ, Bill. What can I say? I'm sorry mate.' McKendrick shrugged.

'Yes, well, that's the way it is. She hasn't long to go. Maybe a couple of weeks, if she's lucky. Or unlucky, depending on how you look at it.'

'She's here? Not in hospital?'

'Yes, she's here.'

'And you're looking after her?'

'Yes, my sister comes over when I need to go out. The married one from Walthamstow. Don't know where the other one is. Little bleeder. Never writes.' Lorrimar leaned back

36

and thought for a moment.

'What happens when we do the job?'

'I was hoping it wouldn't be until after . . . until she'd gone.' McKendrick looked at Lorrimar. 'That's why you're here, it's on soon isn't it?'

'Saturday.'

'Sod it.'

'Do you want out Bill? I can get Eddie in instead. I'll see you're alright. Ten per cent of my cut. Can't speak for the others.'

'No, you can't bring Eddie in this late. You'd have to delay it, and, if you do that, you might as well delay it for me until after she's gone. No, if Saturday is the right day for it, then Saturday it is. She's barely conscious most of the time anyway Dave. Some pills she has. Painkillers they are, keeps her under. She probably won't know I'm gone.'

'Okay Bill, it's up to you. On Saturday, once we're settled in you can ring here. Give your sister the number. She can call you if . . . well, she can call you.'

'Yes, right. I'll see you Saturday then Dave.' The two men stood up and Lorrimar reached out and lightly tapped the other man with his clenched fist.

'Yes. See you mate.' He led the way back to the door that opened into the courtyard. Outside he hesitated for a moment. 'Does Mannion know? About your Mum. Did you tell him?'

'No, nobody else knows, just you, outside my sister and the neighbours.'

'Right, okay Bill. I'll pick you up here about half past six, Saturday morning. Right?'

'Right.' Lorrimar walked out of the courtyard to his car and opened the door. He drove the short distance to the Bull's Head, went in and bought a large scotch. He leaned against the bar and thought about things. If Mannion did not know about the old woman's illness, then there was still an unanswered question, why had McKendrick been selected? It didn't make any kind of sense. He shrugged and finished his drink. Whatever it was that Mannion was up to, it would come out eventually and, in the meantime, all that mattered was that he kept his eyes open. Wide open. And with Hart alerted there was little danger that Mannion would be able to pull something that would catch them unprepared. He walked back to his car and drove steadily into the West End. The nervous tension was building up in his stomach and he headed for the Longboat. The girl would be there, Linda Hooper. That would be one way of relieving the tension.

CHAPTER FOUR

It had rained heavily throughout Friday evening and well into the early hours of Saturday morning, but shortly after Lorrimar had finished dressing and was sitting in the small kitchen of his flat drinking coffee, the rain stopped. He finished the coffee and rinsed the cup under the tap before wiping it dry and replacing it in the cupboard. He picked up his Gucci grip and turned out the lights before opening the door. He didn't look back into the room, he had already checked everything twice over and knew there was nothing there that would tell anyone anything, other than things that would not matter.

He put the grip into the boot of the Daimler that was parked in a turning off Dorset Street and started the engine. He sat for a moment and then selected drive and pressed the accelerator. As the car moved off he felt the remaining dregs of tension slip from him. It had always been the case, whatever the job, however difficult or dangerous, once it was under way he operated smoothly and easily. He saw only two other vehicles on the journey to Hart's flat and he arrived outside the converted house at two minutes before six. He walked up the stairs, not to save the extra energy of running, but to arrive at Hart's door at precisely six o'clock. Hart was waiting for him, the door open and three suitcases stood just inside the flat. Neither man spoke and Lorrimar picked up the two smallest cases and turned away. Behind him he heard Hart close the door and follow him down the stairs. The cases were in the boot of the blue car and they were halfway along Kensington Palace Road before either man spoke. Lorrimar knew that Hart's pre-job nerves were always taut and he let the silence go on, knowing that when Hart was ready to speak he would and that until then he was best left alone.

'Sleep much?' Hart asked.

'Not a lot,' Lorrimar said. In fact he had slept eight hours, going to bed at nine and not waking until five but he felt that a small lie would do no harm.

'Neither did I,' Hart admitted. 'I should be over that kind of thing by now.'

'It doesn't matter now does it.' Lorrimar said. 'That's the last time you'll lose sleep over a job.' Hart laughed quietly.

'I bloody hope so,' he said. Lorrimar did not answer and for several minutes they sat in silence as the car purred quietly through the quiet, dark streets. They had crossed the river before Hart spoke again.

'You reckon Bill will be able to concentrate on things?' Lorrimar had told Hart about McKendrick's mother's illness the previous night in a brief non-committal telephone conversation.

'I think so. Poor sod, he worships her you know.'

'Yes. I know.' Hart thought for a moment. 'He was certain Mannion didn't know?'

'He didn't tell him, but it's always possible Mannion could have found out. He has a long nose.'

'It would make me feel easier if I knew Mannion did know.'

'Me too. Maybe we'll find out before much longer.' When Lorrimar drove slowly past the window of the flat in Grove Road he saw McKendrick looking out at them, the net curtains pulled to one side. As the car passed, the curtain dropped and Lorrimar turned the car and stopped, waiting. In a few moments the small figure came out through the archway and crossed to the car. Hart reached behind him and opened the door and McKendrick climbed in with his small suitcase clutched under his arm. Almost before the rear door had closed the Daimler was moving off. They had recrossed the river and were approaching Knightsbridge before McKendrick spoke.

'Does Jim know?' he asked. Lorrimar nodded his head in silence.

'Yes, I'm very sorry Bill. She's a grand old girl,' Hart said. Somehow the oddly dated words sounded sincere and McKendrick

41

nodded.

'Yes, she is. Christ, she would have got a charge out of this caper if she'd known about it.'

'You didn't tell her then,' Lorrimar said, with a faint tug of alarm in his chest.

'No, couldn't risk it. Not with the drugs she's on. You never can tell.'

'Good. The sister there?'

'Yes, she'll make out alright. She thinks I'm away to the car auctions. I told her I'd 'phone her tonight and give her a number where she can reach me. That's what you said, isn't it Dave?'

'Yes. Mind you, in a couple of days she'll know where you are without any need for a telephone number. Once the TV and newspaper boys are on the job.'

'Unless the law puts a blanket on it.' Hart put in.

'They might do, but the way we're playing it there won't be any need for secrecy.'

'You're right, but you and me and the law don't always think alike.' Lorrimar slowed the car and turned into Montpelier Place and checked his watch.

'Two minutes early,' he remarked. 'Shall we wait or shall I go over and knock on his door?'

'No need,' Hart said. 'He must be eager, here he comes now.' The three men sat in silence watching the figure hurrying towards them. Mannion was carrying a large and heavy-looking suitcase. Lorrimar glanced at Hart.

42

'He'll want that in the boot,' he said. He slipped from his seat and walked round the front of the car to meet Mannion. He reached out a hand for the case. I'll put it in the back for you,' he said, taking the case out of Mannion's hand. 'You get in, it's enough to freeze you.' He turned away and fiddled with the boot key until Mannion was inside the car, then he swung open the lid and added the case to the others already there.

The sky behind them was beginning to lighten as they joined the motorway leading out of the city and Lorrimar kept his speed down to a steady fifty, a random police check or radar trap now would have caused them more problems than they could have dealt with. When they had left the motorway Lorrimar dropped his speed to forty and kept at that until they reached Lower Assendon. At a few minutes past eight he turned into the road leading to Fenton and drove straight through the village centre, taking the Stonor road at the fork. Two miles beyond the fork he stopped and turned the car using a farm track entrance to negotiate the narrow road. He drove back into Fenton and turned hard left around the Fenton Oak and onto the Fawley Road. Two miles along the road he repeated the turn and headed back into the village. They had seen no other vehicles. This time he drove straight through as if going back towards Lower Assendon but turned off to the

43

left into Remenham Lane. Just past the footpath that led up to the rear of Fenton Hall he stopped and turned the Daimler, using a level stretch of grass beneath trees that were the southern extremity of the woods that lay behind the Hall. Lorrimar and McKendrick climbed out and Lorrimar opened the boot. He unlocked one of Hart's suitcases and took out the single-action Beretta and a spare clip. McKendrick dropped his small suitcase into the boot and took the weapon and the ammunition from Lorrimar. He pushed them into his overcoat pocket and looked at his watch.

'Eight thirty-five,' he said. Lorrimar checked his watch.

'Right. See you mate.' He waited until McKendrick had disappeared up the footpath leading to the Hall before climbing back into the Daimler. He sat looking down the lane towards the road that led from Fenton to Lower Assendon. They saw lights pass the road end and Lorrimar checked his watch again. 'Eight forty-five,' he said. 'On the dot.' They waited and then five minutes later the lights appeared again, this time heading towards Fenton. 'And there he goes back again. Going home to Fawley for his bacon and eggs.'

'Sure it's the copper?' Mannion asked.

'It's a Landrover and it had a blue light on the top of the cab. What more do you want,' Hart said irritably.

'Okay, okay,' Mannion said. 'Don't get bitchy.' Hart started to turn round in his seat and Lorrimar put out a restraining hand.

'Alright,' he said. 'Keep it down. Talk when we have to, the rest of the time, keep it shut. Both of you. Right.' Hart turned back and glared out of the windscreen. Lorrimar kept his hand on his arm until he felt him relax. He glanced into his rear-view mirror at Mannion and saw clearly the sheen of perspiration on the fat man's forehead. Mannion looked into the mirror and saw Lorrimar's eyes on him. He grinned humourlessly and Lorrimar wondered for the hundredth time what it was that had made Mannion include himself on the operational team. Ten minutes later they saw the red post office van pass the lane end.

'That just leaves the milkman,' Lorrimar said, opening the door. He opened the boot and took three more weapons from the case. He climbed back into the car and handed the small, neat, five-shot Smith & Wesson to Mannion. He handed one of the .44 Smith & Wessons to Hart and slipped the second into his overcoat pocket. He started the car and drove slowly down the hill. About twenty yards short of the road junction he stopped and they waited, the engine noise barely audible. After a few moments they heard clearly the sound of the milk van and then the white-painted Ford Transit came into view and passed the road end. Immediately Lorrimar put the Daimler in forward and turned right into Fenton Lane. He glanced in his rear-view mirror as he did so and saw the back of the white van, then it was hidden from sight as he turned the Daimler into the right hand bend. He slowed as the entrance to the Hall came into sight and turned onto the gravel drive. The wide tyres of the Daimler crunched on the gravel as they moved up the slight incline. As they reached the path that led to the cottage occupied by the housekeeper and her husband, all three men glanced to their right. Lights were on in one of the upstairs room.

'Breakfast in bed,' Lorrimar remarked.

'Some people don't know they're born,' Hart said.

'You'll soon be having all the breakfasts in bed you can manage old son,' Lorrimar said.

The drive sloped more steeply as they approached the Hall and Lorrimar swung the car to the left and parked directly in front of the three steps that led up to the front door. Ahead of them the wet lawn stretched away towards the north, broken only by flower beds and a small shrubbery. Beyond, the neatly cropped lawn gave way to longer grass where the grounds sloped away towards the village and Lorrimar could just make out the Fenton Oak, half-screened by the buildings at Home Farm. The three men climbed out of the Daimler and moved up the steps, Lorrimar in the lead, Hart behind him to his left and Mannion to the right. Lorrimar rang the bell. They waited, listening to the sound echoing through the house.

Saturday mornings were one of the more pleasant times in the life of Sir James Garroway. He liked the quiet of the house, his wife always slept late and so too, usually, did Belinda, his younger daughter. Sarah, when she was there, was an early riser but she knew her father well enough to stay out of his way. Deliberately, he did not take a newspaper at weekends, it was enough to have to read the Times and the Financial Times every working day without having to plough through several thousand words at the weekends too. He generally made himself tea and toast and sat alone, quiet, in the kitchen. The customary cooked breakfast he would start later, before calling his wife. The routine had been in operation for twelve years, since they had moved into Fenton Hall in fact. The Hall had been one of the first properties Sir James had bought, when he had begun to turn his father's small but useful life insurance policy into a fortune. Before he had become Sir James and was just plain James Garroway, a man in his mid-forties and already talked of as a man to watch in the city. The twelve years that had followed had shown that, for once, the talkers had been right. Now, two years short of his self-imposed retirement age of sixty, he was a millionaire several times over and most of the time even he had difficulty in keeping track of the incredible empire he had built up, not just in England but over most of Europe and the Far East. Unlike many of his contemporaries he refused point-blank to work outside normal office hours, believing that he was a better man for keeping work and relaxation in two air-tight compartments. The fact that, unlike most of his contemporaries, he was still fit and richly successful seemed to confirm that his way was right.

He sipped at his tea and stared out of the window to the trees rising damply at the edge of the lawn. He glanced at his watch, he had ten more minutes of seclusion before he would be ready to start his wife's breakfast. The ringing of the doorbell was unexpected and unwelcome. He waited for a moment, half-hoping that the caller would go away. The bell rang again. He put down his tea cup and stood up. He went out of the kitchen door and walked through the short passage that led into the wider hallway. He unlocked and opened the heavy front door. The man standing there was a couple of inches shorter than Sir James' six feet, he was dressed in a dark overcoat, no hat and his set face under dark wavy hair, looked hard and ruthless, the drooping black moustache seeming an almost frivolous addition. The man's hands were in his pockets. Garroway raised his eyebrows interrogatively and as he did so he saw the two men behind the first man. One, tall and thin and dressed in an off-white calf-length coat of some kind of hide with fur collar and cuffs; the other, shorter, expensively dressed and, despite the cold air, sweating profusely. Both men had their hands in their pockets too. For no reason he could think of, then or later, Sir James knew he was in danger and started to close the door but the first man stepped forward and as he did so his hands came out of his pockets. One held a gun.

'No sound,' the dark-haired man said. The other men came in behind him, one closed the door and locked it, the other crossed straight to the sitting-room door. He opened it and nodded his head at the dark-haired man. 'In there,' the man said and prodded Sir James in the chest with the muzzle of the weapon. Inside the room the three men studied Sir James. 'Sit down if you want,' the first man said. Sir James shook his head. 'Please yourself. Wife still in bed?' Garroway nodded. 'The girls?' Garroway hesitated, his mind racing ahead trying to decide several things at once. 'The girls, Belinda and Sarah. Where are they?' That told Garroway that whatever the men wanted they were well prepared.

'Belinda is still in bed,' he said. 'Sarah isn't here. She lives in London.' The dark-haired man's eyes flickered sideways at the fat man. The fat man nodded his head.

'She's coming later though, isn't she? Due here about twelve-thirty.' Garroway nodded slowly, mentally noting that the fat man's knowledge was excellent and that the other two men hadn't known that last fact. He filed the observation away. He wasn't sure how, but he felt it would have a use later. He also noted that whether or not the others knew about the absence of his elder daughter they didn't let the new information disturb them. They were professionals and Garroway switched his mind into high gear. He had a battle on his hands and he was clever enough to know that whatever the game was, the stakes this time were higher than any he had played for before.

CHAPTER FIVE

Cleaning at the Fenton Oak was normally done by two women from the village but on that Saturday morning only one had turned up for work, the other apparently laid low with 'flu. Simon Arne told the cleaner to concentrate on the bar and the dining room and to leave the bedrooms until the following week.

'We've only one booking for the weekend. An old fellow on his own, I'll give his room a dust round myself,' he told her. 'I'm giving him the one that was let last week, you cleaned it out and changed the bedding last Monday didn't you?'

'Yes, that's right Mr. Arne, we gave it a real good clean.'

'Good,' Arne said and went up the stairs. Since the death of his wife, several years before, he had managed for himself so far as had been possible. That meant that he cleaned his own rooms at the inn and he cooked his own breakfasts and lunches, and on Mondays, when the dining room was normally closed, he cooked his dinner too. He did his own laundry and generally avoided letting himself fall into any of the traps he had seen other middle-aged widowers fall into. His staff were generally reliable and he knew they were all a little afraid of him, not in any physical sense but they certainly went in fear of his tongue. As for the regulars, they were friendly towards him, as he was towards them, but just as he never opened himself, so they too kept well short of real friendliness. He told himself that his ways were as a result of his wife's death, but inside he knew that it wasn't the case, he had never been free and easy with people. He believed firmly in place. Everything and everybody had a place and that place should always be kept and observed. He knew he was regarded as something of an anachronism by most of the people he knew and he knew they were probably right. Not that he was quite as bad as many thought, he had heard one or two people comment that he wanted to see conscription brought back, that and birching and capital punishment. None of it was true because he was only too well aware of the other side of those particular coins.

His war service had been long and honourable, volunteering at the start of the second world war he had risen to captain by 1945 and had stayed on, both he and his wife liking the life. Korea had brought the first souring of his taste for the army and by the time that war was over he was thinking of retirement. Keeping a pub had been a standard joke among most of his immediate colleagues and he had surprised himself as well as the others by being the only one to actually do it. His gratuity and his savings and his wife's money—she had occupied the time when he was on overseas duty by working as a nurse—had been more than enough to buy the freehold of the Oak. They had bought it in 1960 and the world had suddenly seemed a happier place. Then two years later his wife had been killed in a motor accident and it was a disaster beside which everything he had experienced in his life until then faded into insignificance. He had set aside his instinctive reaction to sell the Oak and had stayed on, using it as a life-raft, until gradually the pain had faded and he began again to enjoy life. But the enjoyment was at a different level and he was never able to relax completely with anyone as he had with his wife. Now fifty-eight, he had begun to toy idly with the thought of retirement, but there was nothing he wanted to do, nowhere he wanted to visit, or to live and most important of all, no one with whom he would be able to share that retirement. So he stayed and applied himself, as he had since leaving the army, to the efficient organisation of the Fenton Oak.

The room he was preparing didn't need much doing to it and he finished in less than fifteen minutes. He opened the window to freshen the air and glanced up the hill towards the Hall. He could see the blue car quite clearly but at that distance he wasn't able to see whether it was a Jaguar or a Daimler. He wondered who could be visiting the Garroways that early on a Saturday morning. Sir James' slightly anti-social habits were a common topic in the bar. Arne never joined in. He had met Sir James and Lady Garroway a few times, he supplied the Hall with spirits and beer and on two occasions he had catered for garden parties. He liked Garroway, he respected him, not so much for making his money but for the way in which he organised his life. The efficiency of it impressed him. He was on his way back down to see how the cleaner was coping when he reflected that the last guest in that room had driven a pale blue Daimler. It seemed to be a completely irrelevant thought.

Fenton Hall was not very old as country houses go. Built around 1800 it had a square simplicity that suited Garroway. It was comparatively small, not many rooms but they were large and airy with high ceilings. On either side of the central entrance hall were rooms with windows facing towards the sweep of the lawn that ran down the hill to the road. The room to the left was the dining-room and that to the right, where Sir James and the three armed men were, was the sitting-room. Most of the furniture was Georgian, in keeping with the house, but there were two twentieth-century interlopers, a television set and a radio and record-player, both housed in expensively reproduced period cabinets. Garroway and the man who was clearly the leader, still stood, the fat man had dropped into an armchair. The thin man had left the room after asking where the keys to the Rolls-Royce and the garage were.

'I think we should all sit down,' the dark-haired man said and this time there was an authority in his voice that Garroway decided should be observed. It was too early to risk antagonising any of them, risks might be taken later when he knew what it was they wanted. He sat down and the other man sat on the arm of a chair facing him. He put the gun away and Garroway glanced at the fat man. His gun was out of sight too. 'Don't get any ideas,' the dark-haired man said. He took off his overcoat and laid it across his knees so that the pocket with the gun was uppermost. It pulled the coat out of shape and Garroway didn't doubt that it could be taken out quickly and, if necessary, used without hesitation. 'Time for introductions, my name is Lorrimar, Dave Lorrimar, but I don't expect we'll get that friendly. This is Ken Mannion. The other guy is Jim Hart. Obviously we know who you are.' Lorrimar stretched out his legs. There was an air of total confidence about him and Garroway felt his own confidence slipping. 'Any minute now your good lady wife will start to wonder where her breakfast is. And then there's the kid, Belinda. We'd better be ready for them hadn't we.' He looked speculatively at Garroway. 'You probably won't believe this at the moment, but we have no wish to harm any of you. Do as you are told, exactly as you are told, and no one need get hurt, step out of line and we crack down hard. Bloody hard.' Garroway nodded his head. He believed the man. He looked at the fat man whose eyes quickly slid away and knew that this was another area in which the fat man and his colleagues differed. The fat man did not have the same regard for the safety of the Garroways as did the man who called himself Lorrimar. 'So,' Lorrimar went on. 'When they come down you will call them in here. There may be a bit of hysteria and tears and then we'll talk. That way I have to say things just once. Right?' Garroway thought rapidly. He found the most disturbing thing was the fact that the man had introduced himself and had named his colleagues. The names could easily have been false, but there had been no attempt to hide their faces. He tried to think what kind of criminal act could be prefaced by a businesslike naming of names. He failed to think of anything. 'I said, right?' Lorrimar said, his voice hard. Garroway started.

'Yes, I understand. I, we will all do as you say.' He didn't add that they had little choice. His mind raced on trying to find an answer and then suddenly he registered a fact that had remained, for some unaccountable reason, in his subconscious. He knew that he had gone pale at the thought, but he said nothing. It was possible, it had to be possible, that the men were not here for that reason. They couldn't have known, as well informed as they so obviously were, they couldn't have known. It had to be a coincidence that they had chosen this particular Saturday for whatever it was they wanted.

All three men heard the noise from the hall, the fat man jumped up, but Lorrimar stayed where he was.

'Okay Ken, it's only Jim.' The door opened and the tall, thin man looked in.

'Okay Dave,' he said. 'Everything is in. I'll put the gear in the dining-room for now.'

'Right,' Lorrimar said. 'Then you'd better deal with the telephone.'

'Okay.' Hart disappeared again.

'Just the two telephones,' Lorrimar said conversationally to Garroway. 'One in the breakfast-room and an extension in the dressing-room off your bedroom.' Garroway nodded his head. The door opened again and Hart slipped in.

'Someone's moving about upstairs,' he said. 'Sounds like the kid.' Lorrimar stood up.

'Get up,' he said to Garroway. 'Just take it easy and we won't frighten her.' He motioned to Garroway and the two men walked towards the door. Garroway noted that Lorrimar had left his overcoat, with the gun still in the pocket, behind on the chair arm. He glanced at the other men. Hart had a gun like Lorrimar's in his hand and the fat man, Mannion, had a small revolver clutched in his. He forced himself to relax and opened the door. The staircase came down on to the short passageway that ran between the hall and the kitchen and although they could hear the girl, she was out of their sight until she reached the floor level. Belinda Garroway was twelve years old, she had her father's high forehead and deep-set grey eyes, but unlike him she was very blonde and her long straight hair hung down almost to her waist. She had a faint line of freckles across her cheekbones and she had a wide straight mouth that rarely smiled.

She was a serious, bookish girl. She saw her father and started to speak and then realised there was another man there too.

'Good morning Daddy,' she said and looked enquiringly at Lorrimar.

'Good morning darling,' Garroway said. 'This is, er, Mr. Lorrimar. He's a, er, he has called to see me on some business.'

'Hello Belinda,' Lorrimar said. The girl looked at him unsmilingly.

'Hello,' she said after a moment. Garroway looked at Lorrimar, unsure what to say or do.

'We were just going into the kitchen to make coffee,' Lorrimar said. 'Now you're here maybe you'll make it for us.' The girl nodded her head.

'Alright,' she said. Lorrimar turned to Garroway and lowered his voice.

'Tell her to go and call her mother.'

'Belinda,' Garroway called. 'See if your mother is awake first. Tell ... ask her to come into the sitting-room.' The girl made a great show of exasperation at adult peculiarities and turned and ran noisily up the stairs. The two men waited in the passageway at the foot of the stairs until Belinda reappeared and came back down the stairs.

'She's coming,' she said and went into the kitchen. Lorrimar heard her filling a kettle and then heard the clatter of crockery. It was two or three minutes before Lady Garroway came down the stairs. Obviously her daughter had told her about the visitor and she betrayed no surprise at seeing Lorrimar, not even that he and her husband should be standing waiting for her at the foot of the stairs.

Phyllis Garroway was tall, even in the low-heeled shoes she was wearing she was the same height as Lorrimar. Younger than her husband by almost seven years, she was still slim and attractive, having been blessed with a fine bone structure and a metabolism that did not cause problems of weight. Her hair was fair with only the slightest streaks of grey showing through. Her eyes were grey and she had the habit of looking directly at the person to whom she spoke, a habit that made many think her imperious. In fact she was slightly nervous in company, even after the many years of her husband's success, and her slightly aggressive attitude towards people was a defence against that nervousness. She looked directly at Lorrimar as she came down the stairs and stopped on the last step causing him to look up at her.

'James, I didn't know you were expecting anyone.'

'No dear, this was unexpected,' Garroway kept his voice as neutral and as natural as he could. Now that his wife and his younger daughter were within range of the guns of the three strangers, he was desperately anxious to avoid anything that would cause alarm. 'Perhaps

59

we can go into the sitting-room, then I can introduce you properly to our visitors.' His wife raised her eyebrows.

'Visitors?'

'Yes. The others are in the sitting-room.' Garroway turned away and walked back down the hall and after only the slightest hesitation his wife followed him. Lorrimar walked softly down the hall behind Lady Garroway. Mentally he checked over the programme. Nothing overlooked so far and, with the exception of the absence of the elder daughter, nothing unexpected had occurred. He chewed over that particular matter and the undoubted fact that Mannion had known that Sarah Garroway would not be arriving until twelve-thirty. He ran over the possible dangers inherent in her late arrival and found none that might prove serious. Even so, had they known, they would have postponed the operation until another weekend. That meant only one thing, Mannion had wanted them here on this particular Saturday. His feeling that Mannion was planning something he knew nothing about grew into a certainty. He would have to arrange to talk to Hart soon. And the way the job was planned, with only four of them here, that would be difficult. As that thought entered his mind he suddenly knew why Mannion had kept the team down to four. With McKendrick outside the house there would be few opportunities for private conferences. Mannion had planned well. Lorrimar began to consider the possibilities of aborting. So far they had committed no offence of any consequence. Unauthorised possession of firearms and threatening Garroway with a firearm, but the chances were that nothing could be made to stick. He was still thinking of that when Garroway reached the sitting-room door and paused. The door opened and Mannion stood there. His gun was out of sight although both Garroway and Lorrimar saw and identified the bulge where his jacket clung close to his heavy body. Garroway went in and his wife and Lorrimar followed. Hart immediately went out of the room and Lorrimar motioned to Garroway to sit down. Lady Garroway saw the gesture and her inkling that all was not as it should be, hardened. She turned to her husband.

'I think you had better explain what is happening James,' she said.

'I . . .' Garroway began to speak but Lorrimar interrupted.

'Perhaps it will be better if I explain Sir James,' he said smoothly. He turned to Lady Garroway.

'You are being held prisoner.' His voice was quiet and some of the impact of the words was lessened. He waved his hand to encompass Mannion who had sat down again. 'My friends and I are holding you, your husband and your daughter, Belinda, that is. We shall also hold your daughter, Sarah, when she arrives.' Lady Garroway turned to her husband, her expression combining her normal veneer of calm, surprise and just the faintest beginnings of fear.

'James...' Her husband reached out to touch her.

'Sit down, dear,' he said. He made her sit on the settee that faced the high fireplace and he sat next to her, his hand still resting on her arm. 'What this man has said is true. They are armed. All three of them.' His wife looked at Lorrimar and Mannion. Lorrimar picked up his overcoat and slid the Smith & Wesson from the pocket. He laid it on the chair beside him. Brandishing it would alarm her unnecessarily. Just the sight of it should be sufficient to show her that it was really happening.

Phyllis Garroway's reaction at seeing the weapon the dark-haired man had produced was one of confirmation rather than alarm and her only concern at that moment was for the safety of her daughter.

'Where is Belinda?' she asked.

'She's in the kitchen. Making coffee,' her husband said. The unexpected reply brought the first strong reaction she had felt so far, one of acute relief. At that same instant there was a light knocking at the door. Only Mannion responded. He clambered hastily to his feet pulling at the small, snub-nosed revolver that was jammed into the waistband of his trousers. Lorrimar moved swiftly to the other man.

'Relax Ken,' he said. 'It'll be the girl. Take it easy.' He crossed to the door and opened it. Belinda stood there with a tray in her hands. She came into the room and stood the tray on a small table. She looked at Mannion and then looked pointedly at the number of cups she had placed on the tray. Then, she looked back at Mannion and saw the gun in his hand. She looked at her parents and then walked over to her mother and stood there, uncertainty appearing in her demeanour for the first time.

'Sit down Belinda,' her mother said, her voice calm and steady. The door opened again and Hart came back into the room.

'Okay Dave,' he said. 'I've disconnected the upstairs telephone and reconnected it in the dining-room next to the main instrument. And I've added an extra bell on a trailing lead so we're sure to hear it wherever we are in the house.'

'Okay,' Lorrimar said. He looked at Hart and then let his glance flicker sideways to Mannion. The fat man was looking at the Garroways and Lorrimar let his eyes ask Hart a question. Hart moved his eyes upwards. Lorrimar nodded. Sir James did not miss the exchange. He added the observation to the others he had already made; meaningless though they were he was astute enough to realise that there was already a split in the ranks of the interlopers, how deep he had no way of knowing. Neither did he know whether it was something that he could turn to his advantage, but so far he had little else to cling to for comfort.

Lorrimar walked back to the chair he had been using and again sat on the arm. Hart moved another chair close to the window and positioned it so that he could see down the slope of the lawn and the drive towards the housekeeper's cottage and beyond it to the road. Lorrimar smiled at the girl.

'Thank you for the coffee,' he said. He reached over and picked up a cup. 'Jim. Coffee?' Hart turned round.

'Please,' he said. Lorrimar smiled again at the girl.

'Take my friend a cup,' he said. The girl looked at her father who nodded his head. She picked up a cup from the tray and walked across to where Hart was sitting. She handed the cup to him and walked back and sat down again between her father and mother, unsmiling, gravely watching Mannion and the gun that was still in his hand. Lorrimar followed her eyes.

'Put it away Ken,' he said quietly. Mannion looked up startled. Then, flushing slightly, he did as Lorrimar had said. 'Right,' Lorrimar said. 'Time for explanations.' He looked at Garroway. 'Sorry the girl has to stay in here but there are only the three of us and we can't let her wander around can we?' Garroway found himself beginning to admire the control of the other man. His calm and authority were far more impressive than if he had waved the gun in their faces. Less frightening perhaps, but just as powerful. Lorrimar turned to Lady Garroway. 'I've already introduced myself to your husband,' he started conversationally. 'My name is Lorrimar, Dave Lorrimar. This is Ken Mannion and over there is Jim Hart. We are all armed and as I've already said we are holding you here.' He paused and looked at Garroway. 'We require your husband to do certain things. Provided he does as we ask then there is no reason why we should not leave here on Monday night, maybe Tuesday morning at the latest. You and your daughters will be coming with us but we expect to release all of you very soon afterwards. There is no reason,' he paused again and then repeated his last words, emphasising them carefully, 'there is no reason why anyone should be harmed. But, if you do not do as you are told, exactly as you are told, then harm will be done. I assure you of that.' His voice had changed and the last words were dropped, cold, into the air. Lorrimar leaned forward and replaced his coffee cup on the tray.

'Where do you plan to hold us?' Lady Garroway asked abruptly. Lorrimar looked at her, surprised at the apparent irrelevance of the question.

'Here,' he said.

'Until Monday?'

'Yes.' He looked at her curiously and saw the look that passed between her and her husband. There was something there that he could not understand. He flicked a glance at Hart and Mannion. Hart was looking out of the window and although he had heard, he had not seen the glance between Garroway and his wife. Mannion was sweating more than ever and refused to let Lorrimar catch his eye. Lorrimar found himself forced to an inescapable and unwelcome conclusion—whatever it was that Mannion was up to, Sir James and Lady Garroway knew more about it than he did himself. It was a conclusion he did not like.

CHAPTER SIX

Sarah Garroway was driving too quickly. She usually did. The dark green Porsche was not a car that liked to be driven in any other way. Everything about it seemed to improve the faster it was driven, the suspension, the steering, the gear box and above all the engine. She held the speedometer needle on ninety as she went down the fast lane of the M4. Her long, blonde hair blew back in the airstream that came in through the open windows. The air was cold and easily won its struggle with the powerful heater that was despairingly blowing hot air up from the bottom of the car. As she approached her turn off she reluctantly eased the car down to a slower speed and checked her rear-view mirror before slipping the car across to the inside lane. She left the motorway and with her speed at just over fifty the heater began to regain some ground from the cold air coming in through the windows. She wound down the window on the nearside of the car even further and the temperature dropped again. She let her eyes fall for an instant onto the suitcase lying on the passenger seat and smiled to herself. The evening dress was by far the most expensive thing she had ever bought, to add to what was far from being an inexpensive wardrobe. But then, dinner that evening was not something for which she could have worn anything other than the very best.

As she approached Henley she decided that she would stop there for some last-minute shopping. She glanced at her watch and decided that she would call the Hall and tell her mother that she would be late for lunch, not that it would really matter, Saturday lunchtime was always a cold snack, especially when the Pearsons were having a weekend off, and it had been necessary to ensure that they were off that particular weekend.

*   *   *

At Lorrimar's insistance the Garroways were having a late breakfast. None of them wanted to eat but he had been determined that no one should go for long without food. Lady Garroway had gone into the kitchen and had made scrambled eggs for herself and her husband. Belinda had decided on cereals and toast and was eating with no apparent lack of appetite. Lorrimar and Hart were also eating toast and drinking more coffee which had been made and stood in the middle of the dining-room table. Lorrimar had vetoed the breakfast-room as being too small, he didn't want them all cramped together, which could lead to problems. Not that he was expecting trouble. So far Garroway had behaved perfectly and his wife was obviously concerned that her daughter should not be harmed, but Lorrimar knew that before long Garroway would begin to flex his muscles. After a while even guns became just pieces of metal. There would come a time when he would have to prove that they were there to be used if it became necessary.

'Okay,' Lorrimar said, pushing aside his plate and his cup and saucer. 'Time we told you what we want.' He reached into his pocket and took out a sheet of paper. He laid it on the table and glanced at it as if refreshing his memory. He looked up at Garroway. 'You've done well,' he

68

said and there was a note of respect in his voice. 'Twelve years ago you started, didn't you? Before that you were just one of the crowd. A bit brighter and maybe a bit richer, but one of the crowd all the same. Now look at you.' He picked up the paper and waved it towards Garroway. 'Property companies, here and in Hong Kong, two firms of international insurance brokers, a half share in a shipping line, interests in manufacturers of cars and electrical goods here and in Europe, and, best of all, five banks, three in London, one in Hong Kong and one in Australia. I expect there's more too, but that's enough to keep any man happy.' His voice hardened. 'And it's more than enough to let you do what we want you to do.' He pointed to the two telephones. 'We'll wait until after your daughter gets here, but then you can make a start. You will place calls to all the executives necessary to enable you to raise liquid cash by Monday afternoon or evening. Where necessary they will raise documents for your signature and you will tell them that you will be in your office at the usual time on Monday morning to sign anything that needs signing. Any documents that have to be signed by more than one director will be kept to a minimum, but I expect your internal safeguards are such that most will have to bear more than just your signature. That can't be helped.' He paused and glanced again at the paper he was holding. 'We have on here the names and telephone numbers of all the executives you will need to call. You will not be allowed to call anyone not on this list. You will not tell them why you want liquid cash, but you can tell them that you will inform them of the reason for your actions when you go to the office on Monday. If you think it is necessary you can even call a board meeting of the holding company for Monday in order to tell them what you want the money for.'

'What will I tell them on Monday?' Garroway asked in bewilderment.

'You will tell them the truth. That your wife and daughters are being held for ransom and that if the money is not forthcoming they will be killed.' There was silence after Lorrimar finished speaking. Garroway struggled with the threat and at the same time part of his brain was beginning to bring forward the names of the men he would need to contact to realise cash at such short notice. His wife was thinking desperately of some way that she could protect Belinda and at the same time warn her other daughter. She looked at her watch. It was past eleven. Sarah would be on her way by now. There seemed to be nothing that she could do. Garroway breathed deeply.

'You haven't said how much,' he said. Lorrimar looked at him, a small smile on his lips. Garroway was going along.

'Four million,' he said. No one spoke for

several minutes. Lady Garroway heard the figure and refused to believe it. Her daughter had stopped taking too much notice of what was being said, she was aware that there was something to fear, but she had seen enough television programmes to inure herself to the realities of the situation. Lorrimar and Hart were both watching Garroway to see his reaction. Mannion sat silently at the table, his thoughts masked from everyone in the room. Garroway heard the figure without much surprise, he had already anticipated a large sum. A million would not have seemed unlikely, and once you were past the million any figure at the front of the noughts was as good as any other. He briefly wondered why not three or six, a number divisible by three, but then his mind switched into gear and began to assess the technical problems that would have to be overcome if the ransom demand was to be met. Then another part of his brain picked out something else that Lorrimar had said.

'You expect me to tell them, my colleagues, why I need the money?'

'You won't be able to raise it otherwise, will you?' Lorrimar said.

'Probably not, but. . .'

'Yes?'

'The more people there are who know, the more difficulty there will be in keeping the facts from the police.'

'Right. We don't expect you to go straight to them but, if they find out, then we're prepared for that.' Garroway shook his head slowly.

'I don't understand.' he said.

'You don't have to,' Mannion cut in harshly. 'Just do as you're told.'

'Okay Ken. Leave it,' Lorrimar said quietly. He turned back to Garroway. 'I imagine you wondered why we made no attempt to hide our faces and why we told you our names. They are our real names by the way. Well, I haven't finished with the demands. Apart from the money there are other things we will need. We want an aircraft laid on for us, at Abingdon, complete with a pilot. We'll give you the details later, but it's a light plane and there are quite a few of them around. You shouldn't have too much difficulty in getting one and there's always a flyer around who's prepared to take a small chance for a large sum of money. How much you pay him will be up to you, but you have our assurance that he will not be harmed ... by us that is. If the police start something then it'll be every man for himself. We shall also need a helicopter to take us from here to Abingdon. It would be useful if the same pilot can fly both machines, saves involving too many people, but if you have to get two men, then do so.'

'A helicopter can't land here, the ground isn't level.'

'No, we're going from here, in your car, as far

as the field beside the churchyard. It's level and clear of trees. The helicopter will land there.'

The two telephones and the extra bell extension that Hart had fitted were standing on the sideboard in the dining-room and when they all rang together the noise startled everyone. Even Lorrimar, who had maintained absolute control over himself, spun round, his hand reaching for his gun. Then he relaxed and grinned self-consciously. He turned back to the Garroways and pointed at Sir James.

'You answer it. I'm picking up the second 'phone. Don't try anything stupid.' He waited until Garroway had his hand on the telephone and then nodded his head. Both instruments were lifted simultaneously and Lorrimar covered his mouthpiece with his hand. It was Sarah Garroway.

'Hello, it's me,' she said. 'I'm in Henley, but I have some shopping to do. I'll be late, about two-ish I should think.'

'That's alright,' Garroway said, watching Lorrimar's face. 'We'll have lunch without you.'

'Yes, I might get something to eat here although I don't know if I'll be able to eat much. It's exciting isn't it?' Lorrimar looked at Garroway, his eyes narrowing.

'Yes,' said Garroway and then hurried on. 'We'll see you later.' He hung up the receiver before his daughter had time to say anything more. He walked back to the chair he had been sitting in. Lorrimar glanced at the others and read nothing in their faces. He re-ran the side of the conversation they had heard through his mind and knew there was nothing there that would cause their minds to race as his was.

'Right,' he said, abruptly reaching a decision. 'Jim, time you gave Sir James the details of the aircraft we want. Ken.' He nodded his head in the direction of the breakfast-room and walked through the opened double doors with Mannion following him. He lowered his voice when Mannion came up to him. 'Go through the ground floor Ken, drawers, cupboards. Jim's already checked upstairs. You're looking for a gun. Living out here it's always possible Garroway keeps something.'

'Not according to the information we have.'

'Maybe not, but we're not taking any chances. Before that make some coffee. There'll be a flask somewhere in the kitchen. Fill it, black, a lot of sugar. Take it out to Bill.'

'Why not ask them where they keep the flask, always assuming there is one.'

'Because they will put two and two together and work out there are more than the three of us. And there's bound to be a flask, everybody has one. Christ, even I have.' Lorrimar waited until Mannion had walked through into the kitchen and then went back to where Hart was talking to Garroway. As Hart was finishing Lorrimar carried four dining chairs over to the door that opened into the hall and stood them in a jumbled heap where they would slow down anyone trying to leave the dining-room in a hurry. Then, when Hart had finished, he drew him away to the breakfast-room. He needed to talk.

CHAPTER SEVEN

Sir James Garroway had mentally detached himself from his surroundings, his conscious mind totally absorbed in the mechanics of arranging to release funds of the magnitude demanded by the three men. Although subconsciously aware that he should be seeking ways to escape from them, he was absurdly intrigued by the problem and he applied himself to the task with enthusiasm. For his wife the reality of their position was much clearer. There were the three of them, helpless and defenceless, and there were three men all armed and all presumably prepared to use their weapons if they did not get what they wanted. Worse, her other daughter would be at the house soon, driving unknowingly into the same captivity. And there was something even worse than that. Something the three men seemed not to know. There had to be a way out. She looked at her young daughter and the beginnings of an idea came into her mind.

Lorrimar and Hart were standing close together at the far end of the breakfast-room. They could hear Mannion as he moved out of the kitchen and opened the door that led from the kitchen into the garden at the rear of the house. The Garroways were still seated at the dining-table, Sir James with his head bent over a note pad on which he was making calculations, the little girl sitting reading a magazine, apparently unconcerned and Lady Garroway her eyes on her husband, but her mind obviously elsewhere. Lorrimar glanced at the case Hart had pushed under the sideboard.

'We'd better find another home for that lot,' he said. 'We want it out of here at least, but not where Mannion can get at it without us knowing.'

'Where?'

'Out in the hall might be best, after the girl gets here.'

'She didn't suspect anything?'

'No, I don't think so, although her old man hung up a bit sharpish.'

'Nerves.'

'Maybe.'

'What do you mean?' Hart asked curiously.

'I'm not sure. She said something about being too excited to eat.'

'Meaning?'

'I don't know. Then there was something she

76

said,' he nodded towards Lady Garroway. 'Earlier, she seemed more concerned that we would be staying here over the weekend. Almost seemed to prefer it if we'd said we were taking them away somewhere.'

'You mean something might be going on here tonight?'

'Could be.'

'What, dinner guests, visitors of some kind?'

'Not dinner guests, they would have kept the housekeeper here if that was the case, not given her the weekend off. Visitors, maybe, but if that's all, why not tell us? They gain nothing by letting their friends walk in here. If they told us we would simply tell them to call up their friends and say they were ill or something.'

'They might not be thinking that clearly.'

'Maybe not, but I doubt it. She isn't dumb and he's a cold fish. Look at him, he's bloody enjoying it.' Lorrimar hesitated. 'Then there's Ken.'

'What about him?'

'When she said that, about us holding them here, he seemed to know what it was that was worrying her.'

'You're sure?'

'Not sure, no, but all things put together I'm sure that something is going to break tonight. We'll need to be alert for it.'

'Time we told Bill, do you think?'

'Yes. Where did you put the other cases, the

ones with the stuff Mannion doesn't know about.'

'They're in the dressing-room off the main bedroom.'

'Okay, I'll deal with them later.'

'Right.' The door from the hall opened and banged against the pile of chairs Lorrimar had arranged.

'Come in through the kitchen Ken,' Lorrimar called and the door closed again and a moment later Mannion reappeared in the kitchen doorway. Lorrimar nodded at Hart who went out through the same door and moments later Lorrimar heard a slight sound as Hart went up the stairs, but Mannion didn't seem to notice.

'What's the idea of the barricade?' he asked.

'Juse in case anyone wanted to make a run for it.'

'Oh. Been having a conference?'

'No,' Lorrimar said easily. 'Just making sure Jim's happy with the arrangements for the aircraft.'

'What now?'

'I think it's time we went back into the sitting-room and made ourselves comfortable,' Lorrimar said.

★   ★   ★

Sarah Garroway had been mildly surprised at her father's abruptness on the telephone, then she had put it from her mind, after all there was no reason why he should not be as nervous as she was. She left the telephone kiosk and climbed back into the Porsche. After some difficulty she found a parking space in the centre of Henley and hurried to the shops.

At the Fenton Oak there was the usual Saturday lunchtime crowd but Simon Arne was able to leave everything to his barman, Peter. He spent the lunch period in the small office behind the bar bringing his accounts book up to date.

CHAPTER EIGHT

When Sarah Garroway arrived at the Hall she was surprised to see her father's car outside the front door. She knew his aversion to leaving the house at weekends, particularly during the winter months. As she stopped her Porsche outside the garage it occurred to her that perhaps he had to go out and that that was the cause of his grumpiness over the telephone. She climbed out of the low car and walked across to the garage door. It was locked and she turned to go back to her car as her garage key was on the same key ring as the car's ignition key.

Hart and Lorrimar were watching her from the sitting-room window.

'She'll see the Daimler,' Hart said.

'Won't matter,' Lorrimar said. 'It won't mean anything to her.' Outside they saw the young woman reach into the car and then, apparently changing her mind about garaging her car, she straightened up with a suitcase in her hand. She closed the car door and walked quickly over to the front door of the house. Lorrimar turned and taking Sir James by the arm, propelled him rapidly into the hall. 'Remember what I told you,' he said. Sir James nodded, unlocked the door and opened it as his daughter came up onto the top step.

'Hello Sarah,' he said. She reached out with her free hand and leaned forward to kiss him. Then she noticed Lorrimar.

'Oh, I didn't see you there for a moment,' she said.

'This is Mr. Lorrimar,' her father said. 'He is here with some colleagues, on a business matter.'

'In that case I'll go straight up to my room. Where is mother?' Lorrimar glanced at Garroway and almost imperceptibly moved his head.

'Your mother is in the sitting-room,' Garroway said. 'I think you should join us first.' His daughter looked at him, her face clouding slightly. Her father's face showed some sign of strain, something that she had seldom seen before, but she said nothing and, leaving her case on the floor, followed him into the room with Lorrimar following behind. Her mother was sitting on the settee with Belinda sitting next to her, still seemingly engrossed in a magazine. Facing them, in one of the armchairs was a fat man, balding and looking ill-at-ease. Another man was standing by the window, tall, thin and, despite the warmth of the centrally heated room, wearing a long overcoat that seemed completely out of place both on him and in the house.

'Please sit down Sarah,' said her father. She moved to sit beside her mother and as she did so she looked closely into Lady Garroway's face and read enough there to tell her that things were far from well. She stopped short and turned.

'Sit down Miss Garroway.' It was the dark-haired man her father had introduced that spoke. His face was hard and there was no doubt that the words were spoken as an order. She looked for guidance to her father and he nodded slowly. She sat down and instinctively reached out a hand to her mother both protecting and seeking protection. Lorrimar nodded at Sir James.

'Sarah,' her father began hesitantly, 'You must do as these men say. They are armed and they are holding us here. We are prisoners.' He stopped and waited. His daughter looked from him to the three men and then her eyes returned to her father.

'What do they want?' she asked.

'Money,' her father said simply. Lorrimar was watching closely and there was undisguised relief on the young woman's face. Like the rest of her family she had been expecting something worse and Lorrimar's brain raced as he tried to determine what it was the family were expecting. He thought fleetingly of taking Mannion into another room and demanding to know what double-game he was playing. He discarded the thought, deciding that instead he would let Mannion continue in the belief that his duplicity was still undetected. There was always the possibility that the Garroways would talk, but he put that thought aside too. Anything that let them think their captors were not as well-informed and organised as they had so far shown, would erode the advantage Lorrimar felt they held.

'That's right,' he said to the young woman. 'Money. Your father will raise a ransom of four million pounds by Monday night. When we have it and are clear of here, the rest of you go free, and unharmed. There's no percentage in hurting anyone so don't worry on that score. All you need to concern yourself about is that you don't cause us any trouble.'

'Where are you planning to hold us?' Sarah asked, repeating almost word for word her mother's earlier question.

'Here,' Lorrimar said. Her response was as he had expected; concern, greater than she had shown when her father had told her what the three men wanted, but also fear. 'Did you have something to eat in Henley?' he asked. She was clearly surprised at the question, exhibiting as it did, concern for her welfare and knowledge of her telephone conversation with her father.

'Yes, thank you,' she said. Lorrimar nodded. He walked over to Hart and nodded. Hart followed him outside the door.

'I'm going outside for a word with Bill,' Lorrimar said softly. 'Before I do I'll slip upstairs and collect the rest of the gear. I'll put the rifles and the hand guns where we can get at them quickly. The rest will be safer outside for now.' Hart nodded.

'I'll see Ken stays in here.'

'Right, then when I come back in we'd better organise them for visits to the bathroom. After that, it'll be time for Garroway to start making his telephone calls.

'Okay. Any ideas yet what, or who, it is they're expecting tonight?'

'No, but there's no doubt about it. There's something or someone coming here tonight. You saw how the girl reacted?'

'Same as the others.'

'Yes.'

'I was thinking...' Hart's voice trailed off.

'What?'

'Maybe the little girl is the best one to ask. The others will probably cover up.'

'Good idea. I'll try later.'

'Not too late. If it's something that is going to cause us trouble, the more warning we have the better.'

'Don't worry about it Jim. With the extra muscle you've got in those cases we can take on an army if we have to.' Hart grinned.

'Let's hope not.'

'Why not? Don't you fancy some large-scale aggro?'

'No I don't and neither do you, you're like me Dave, a quiet life and lots of money's all you want.' Lorrimar grinned.

'Chance will be a fine thing.'

'This time next week we'll be in . . .'

'Cut it out Jim.'

'Eh? Oh, no, don't worry mate, luxury was what I was going to say.'

'Right. I'll see you.' Lorrimar returned to Mannion and leaned close to whisper in his ear. 'Going to check with Bill.'

'What if the telephone rings?' Mannion asked. Lorrimar grunted in annoyance. He had overlooked bringing the telephone through to the sitting-room.

'I'll bring it in here before I go out,' he said. He walked through to the dining-room and carried the extension, with its extra-long lead, across the hall into the other room. He stood the instrument on a small table by the door and went out again. He went softly up the stairs and into the dressing-room off the main bedroom. He carried the two suitcases down into the hall and opened one. He took out the two Russian AKM rifles and the two extra handguns Mannion knew about and after a moment's thought he took them into the small cloakroom opposite the foot of the stairs. Then he picked up the second case and walked through the kitchen and onto the gravel path that surrounded the house. He couldn't see McKendrick, but he waved his hand and moments later he saw the little man hurrying from among the trees at the end of the lawn behind the house.

'How's it going mate?' he asked as McKendrick came up to him.

'Okay Dave, seen nobody and the only thing I've heard was that car that came up to the house earlier. I take it there weren't any problems?'

'No, it was the elder daughter.'

'I thought she was going to be here when we arrived?'

'So did we.' Lorrimar thought for a moment. 'Look mate, we're not sure but we think, that is Jim and I, we think there is something going on here tonight. We don't know what, maybe it's just visitors, maybe something else. Anyway, whatever it is, the Garroways are more worried about it than they are about us wanting four million pounds out of the till.' He hesitated and McKendrick looked at him curiously. 'We think Mannion knows about it as well. We think he's planning some kind of deal.' McKendrick nodded his head slowly.

'Well as long as we know, we can be ready.' Lorrimar hefted the case he still had in his hand.'

'There's some insurance in here,' he said. 'Insurance Mannion doesn't know about. Find somewhere to hide it Bill, not too far from the house, we might need it in a hurry.' McKendrick took the case from Lorrimar, gasping slightly at the unexpected weight. He looked at the bigger man for a moment.

'If you brought this with you then you were expecting trouble before,' he said.

'Yes, sorry mate. We weren't sure, we just had a feeling, that's all. What has happened since we got here has confirmed it. Before that there didn't seem any point in giving you something else to worry about.'

'Right, okay Dave. I'll find a home for it. When can I call home?'

'We'll be letting them all use the bathroom soon, I'll tip you the wink and you can slip in and call your sister.'

'Okay.'

'Anything you need?'

'Not yet, fix some more coffee when you have time,' McKendrick said. 'I'll bring the flask over and stand it outside the kitchen door.'

'Something in it this time?'

'Nice idea, but better not. There'll be time for that later.'

'You're right. What about food?'

'Later.'

'Don't know how you stand the cold mate. It's bloody freezing out here.'

'Years of practice that's what does it.' Lorrimar grinned as the little man walked away, leaning over to counteract the dead weight of the suitcase. He turned and hurried back inside the house. He went straight to the sitting-room and began to organise everyone to the upper floor. He had settled on the master bedroom as being the most suitable. The biggest of the upstairs rooms, it was at the back of the house with its two windows both looking over the lawn to the line of trees already beginning to blur as the light faded. There was the advantage of the dressing-room that opened off it, the room was small and windowless and would serve as close confinement for any or all of the Garroways should that become necessary. Lorrimar sent Hart into the bathroom to make the window difficult to open without noise, then, leaving Mannion in charge of the family, he slipped down the stairs and waved through the kitchen window. McKendrick came into the house and followed Lorrimar softly down to the dining-room. Lorrimar left him there for a moment and carried the spare telephone back from the sitting-room.

'Okay mate, call your sister.' He left him there and went down to the kitchen and filled a kettle with water and switched it on. The kettle had boiled and he was filling the flask McKendrick had left beside the door when the little man came into the kitchen. 'How is she?' he asked.

'Same. She doesn't know I'm not there which is the main thing. Christ, Dave, I wish I knew if I was doing the right thing. Staying away when she's about to go.'

'It is the right thing Bill. I know it's easy for me to say it, but life is for living. If she knew what was going on she'd want you to be here, setting yourself up for the rest of your life.' McKendrick nodded slowly.

'I expect you're right. That for me?'

'Yes, right, see you later. We'll get some food organised about seven. Unless anything happens before then.'

'Right,' McKendrick opened the door. 'By the way there's a small greenhouse at the back of the garage, inside it, on the right of the door, there's a cupboard. It had plant pots and odds and sods in it. I've cleared them out and I've put the case in there.'

'Okay Bill. See you.'

'See you.' McKendrick closed the door behind him and Lorrimar went back up the stairs.

Hart had finished and they allowed the Garroways to use the bathroom. Lady Garroway asked that she should be allowed to go with her younger daughter and Lorrimar saw no reason to refuse the request. When they were all back in the main bedroom he brought in extra chairs from the other rooms and then looked round to ensure he had overlooked nothing.

'Right,' he said. 'We're leaving you three ladies here for a while. Jim, you stay with them, you,' he pointed at Sir James, 'you come with us.' He turned and went out of the room. Garroway, after a look at his family with what he hoped was a reassuring expression on his face, followed. Mannion closed the door behind them and followed Garroway. Lorrimar led the way to the dining-room. He carried the two telephones to the table and motioned to Sir James to sit at the table. He pushed one of the instruments towards him and took out the list of names and telephone numbers he had shown the financier before.

'Time to start making calls. Who do you want first?'

'Klein.' Lorrimar looked at the list.

'Finance director. Right.' He dialled and waited until the number was ringing and then handed the instrument to Sir James and picked up the second telephone. When the telephone was answered Lorrimar carefully took out the

89

Smith & Wesson and laid it on the table in front of him. Garroway looked at it, then looked up into Lorrimar's eyes. Then he began to speak to the man on the telephone.

CHAPTER NINE

It was past six o'clock when Garroway finished making his telephone calls and Lorrimar, satisfied that good progress had been made, called a temporary halt. He had noted that when Garroway was involved with his associates in the problem of raising the money and in setting up the other parts of the operation, he lost all interest in his immediate surroundings. When the calls were over he became tense again, constantly checking and re-checking his watch. Lorrimar took Sir James back up the stairs to re-join his family and decided that it was time he talked to the younger of the daughters.

'Come along Belinda,' he said amiably. 'You can help me make some tea for us all.' The girl stood up and Lorrimar was slightly concerned that her mother made no attempt to stop her going out of the room with him. He took her down to the kitchen and let her organise cups and saucers and biscuits and cheese and cake. Although he was beginning to feel hungry he was unwilling to let any member of the family become involved in cooking a meal. That could come later when Mannion had made any move that he had planned. He watched the girl, admiring her apparent lack of concern but realised that in all probability she was not fully aware of what was happening. 'What time will your visitors be here?' he asked casually.

'About nine,' she said. He breathed out carefully, unaware until then that he had been holding his breath.

'Both of them?' he asked. She looked up from placing the sugar bowl on to a tray.

'Of course,' she said. 'Grandma and Grandpa always come together.' She turned away and Lorrimar watched her movements, his mind assessing the information. It didn't seem likely; if the parents of Sir James or Lady Garroway were expected there was no reason why the family would have kept it a secret. Had they revealed the information then a telephone call would have been enough to have stalled the visit. It crossed his mind that the girl's grandparents might not be on the telephone, but he discarded that as being unlikely. Anyone as wealthy as the Garroways would not have allowed such a close relative to remain isolated from their children by not having a telephone installed. The alternative to believing Belinda was to disbelieve her which meant that she had been primed to lie. He let his mind flicker back over the events of the day. He had almost given up trying to spot the loophole when he remembered letting the girl and her mother go into the bathroom together. That had to be it. Lady Garroway had taken the opportunity to prime the girl which meant several things to Lorrimar. One was that Lady Garroway was some way ahead of him in her thinking. She had assumed, before they had thought of it, that Belinda was the one member of the family most likely to be questioned by them. It also meant that the visitor or visitors had sufficient status to warrant involving the young girl in the complicated duplicity necessary to carry through the deception. It also told him that whatever time of arrival was scheduled for the visit, it certainly wasn't going to be nine o'clock. Abruptly he decided that he couldn't risk playing the waiting game any longer. He had to know who or what they were up against. The kettle boiled and he filled the teapot and then carried one of the trays upstairs with the girl carrying the second, lighter, tray ahead of him. In the bedroom again he checked his watch. It was seven o'clock. He decided that Sir James would be the best person to talk to but decided to wait a few minutes longer. He whispered to Mannion that he was going to call McKendrick in for a drink and that the family should be kept in the bedroom until the little man was out of the house again. He went back down the stairs and from the kitchen window he waved into the darkness. Moments later McKendrick materialised at the door.

'I want a quick search of the ground floor Bill,' Lorrimar said. 'We're looking for a diary, an address book, any odd bits and pieces of paper that might tell us what's going on here tonight. You start in the sitting-room while I check one of the bedrooms. Then I'll come back down and help you finish off.' He went up to Sarah Garroway's bedroom and checked drawers and wardrobes and came away empty handed. On the way back down the stairs he remembered the suitcase she had been carrying when she had arrived at the house. Earlier he had pushed it into the small cupboard off the passageway between the hall and the kitchen. He now lifted it out and taking it into the kitchen he stood it on the table and snapped open the catches. On the top of the contents was a paper bag marked with the name of a shop in Henley. It contained a new evening bag. He had seen several in his check through her bedroom and to his eye this one seemed neither better nor worse than any of the others. Beneath it was a tissue-paper wrapped evening gown that looked very expensive. There had been several evening dresses in the bedroom too. Nothing else in the case told him anything. He heard McKendrick in the passageway.

'Anything?' he asked.

'No, nothing.'

'Okay Bill. I've had an idea anyway so forget it for now. Ready for anything to eat or drink?'

'Wouldn't mind.'

'Okay, help yourself, keep as quiet as you can, I'm going back upstairs. When you're ready let yourself out. Okay?'

'Right.' Upstairs Lorrimar sat down on one of the spare chairs in the bedroom. He glanced at Hart and winked at him.

'Do either of you want to stretch your legs?' he asked Hart and Mannion together. Hart, alerted by the wink, shook his head and Mannion stood up.

'Yes, I do,' he said. He went out of the room. Lorrimar looked at Sarah.

'Were you planning on a night out?' he said. She started to shake her head, but he went on speaking. 'If you were, then unless you can cancel it easily, you'd better go ahead with it. I don't have to tell you what will happen if you say anything to anyone.' The young woman looked at him in surprise and Lorrimar could see from the expressions that chased across her face that she was working out various possibilities in her mind. He studiously avoided watching her too closely and let his eyes wander instead to her mother and her father. He saw Garroway nod his head very slightly.

'Yes,' she said eventually. 'I am supposed to be going out. Do you really mean I can still go?'

'Yes.'

'Then . . .' she stood up, still uncertain.

'Stay on this floor,' he told her. 'You can use the bathroom and your own room. I'll bring your case up for you. Don't try to go down the stairs without telling me. Or there'll be trouble. Right?' She nodded. He stood up and opened the door for her and followed her to her bedroom and then checked to see if Mannion was in the bathroom. He wasn't and as he turned away he heard him coming up the stairs.

'Okay Ken?' Mannion looked startled, obviously not expecting to see Lorrimar on the landing.

'Yes, sure,' he said.

'The girl's in her room and I've told her she can use the bathroom, she wants to get changed, she's still in the clothes she drove down in and you know what women are.'

'Yes, okay Dave.'

'You stay in there with Jim, I'll be back soon.' He watched the fat man go back into the bedroom and went down to the kitchen to collect the woman's suitcase. The lights were out in the kitchen and he saw McKendrick in the light from the passageway as he went in through the doorway.

'Eating in the dark Bill?'

'That way I can still watch the grounds,' McKendrick said. Lorrimar picked up the suitcase. 'Ken's just been downstairs,' McKendrick went on.

'Yes, did he come in here?'

'No, he just went into the dining-room.' Lorrimar stood the case down again.

'Go on,' he said. The little man's teeth gleamed in the darkness.

'He made a telephone call,' he said.

'Did he now.' Lorrimar pulled a chair out from the table and sat down.

'Yeah, he wasn't on long either. I heard the bell make a noise, that would be the extra bell Jim fixed, either that or it was the extension. Anyway when I heard it I went out of here and down the passageway. I didn't know who it was then of course. I only got a few yards down the hall when the bell sounded again so I shot back in here. I saw Ken come out of the room and then he went into the cloakroom. He was making a bit of a noise in there and when he came out he had the two rifles with him. He came in here.'

'He saw you?'

'No, I went in the corner behind the deep-freeze unit. He didn't put the light on, I figured he wouldn't. He would think I was out there and he wouldn't want me to see him.'

'What did he do with the rifles?' Lorrimar saw McKendrick's teeth gleam again.

'They're in the laundry room. He's covered them with some folded sheets. Dirty ones. No imagination, some people.'

'Well, well, well,' Lorrimar said. 'Okay mate.

When you're ready, slide out of here and you'd better check the gear in the greenhouse. Just in case we run into bother we'd better have it split up. Leave some of it there and put some of it, maybe in the wood at the bottom of the ... no that's too far from the house. Any ideas?'

'There's a vegetable garden over there,' McKendrick waved his arm. 'In the dark nobody will see anything. I'll wrap the gear in some plastic bags there are in the greenhouse.'

'Right. Do that. I've told the girl she can keep a date she has tonight, so you might hear something out front.'

'You're kidding.'

'Yes I am, but she doesn't know I'm kidding and neither does the rest of the family.'

'What are you up to?'

'I want to know who is coming here tonight. I don't reckon any of the Garroways are going to tell me and I'm sure Ken won't. I don't want to find out when they're on the doorstep. I want time to re-organise if I have to.'

'But ...'

'I reckon she will either go for a 'phone, or, more likely, seeing it's late, she'll stop somewhere close and try to head off the visitor. I'll be with her if she does. Only she won't know I'm there.'

'It's a risk Dave.'

'Isn't all of it?'

'I expect so.'

'Okay mate. Oh, and Ken doesn't know anything about anything.'

'Neither do I,' the little man said. He stood up and went out of the door into the garden. Lorrimar went into the dining-room and picked up the telephone extension with its extra-long trailing lead that Hart had fitted. He carried the instrument and Sarah Garroway's suitcase up the stairs with him. He stood the telephone on a small table on the landing. He walked to the bathroom door and tapped at it. There was no reply and he turned and tapped at the adjacent door which was Sarah Garroway's bedroom.

'Who is it?' he heard her say.

'Me, Lorrimar,' he said. The door opened. He handed her the suitcase. He waited on the landing for ten minutes and then tapped again. She was dressed, ready to go out, the new evening dress he had seen in the case looked very good on her despite some slight creasing from its journey in the case. He ran an observant eye over her. In the short time it had taken her to get ready she had done well but there were obvious signs that she had rushed. 'You're ready then,' he said.

'Almost.'

'Let's go,' he said.

'You're coming with me?' Her voice was filled with alarm.

'Me? No. I'm coming to see you don't try to use the telephone and to give you a few words of

98

advice.' She turned away and picked up an evening bag, he noticed that it wasn't the one she had apparently bought especially for the occasion. Then she picked up a fur coat and slipped it over her shoulders. As she came back to where he waited at the door he stopped her. 'I don't want you to go in there to speak to your parents.'

'Why not?'

'One of my mates doesn't think you ought to go. So I don't think we should give him a chance to stop you.' He led the way, moving softly and she followed him. He unlocked and opened the door and they went out into the cold air. He opened the door of the Porsche and helped her in. 'Don't start the engine,' he said. 'Release the handbrake and I'll push it until it's rolling. You should get most of the way down the drive before you need to start the engine, try not to start it until you're almost down at the gate. And go slowly, the tyres on the gravel make a lot of noise.' She nodded her head and he closed the door softly and went round to the back of the car and began to push. As soon as the car was rolling he stepped off the gravelled area onto the lawn. As soon as he was certain she would not be able to see him he set off down the sloping lawn, running swiftly and silently over the grass, his long strides made longer with the help of the incline. He ran at a closing angle to the drive and he easily gained on and passed the car as

Sarah Garroway carefully followed his instructions about moving slowly. He reached the shrubbery that surrounded the entrance to the drive and pushed his way into a clump of rhododendrons and waited. His breathing was still well under control. He watched as the car came nearer and then it stopped. He heard the door open and then she came towards where he waited, she was walking on the grass at the edge of the drive and she made no noise. She passed where he stood and then a short distance further on she stepped into the shrubbery on the opposite side of the drive to him. He could just make out her position helped by the light colour of the dress visible below her coat.

He changed his position carefully and dropped into a crouch, relaxed, he didn't know how long they would have to wait for the visitors and he wanted to be ready.

CHAPTER TEN

Lorrimar had been out of the main bedroom for about half an hour when Mannion needed to go to the bathroom. He left the bedroom door open and after a moment Hart stood up and walked out onto the landing. The Garroways could see him walking up and down, stretching his long arms and legs. Sir James leaned close to his wife.

'I can't hear Sarah,' he said, his voice pitched low. His wife looked at him a flare of panic in her eyes.

'You don't think that other man, Lorrimar, you don't think that he . . .'

'No. No, I'm sure he wouldn't harm her.'

'He said we would all be killed if we didn't do as they said.'

'Yes, but he . . .' Garroway's voice tailed off. 'He might be questioning her,' he said after a moment.

'About . . . ?'

'Yes.'

'Would she tell him the truth?'

'Of course not.'

'Maybe not. I wonder . . .' Lady Garroway's voice faltered.

'What is it?'

'I . . . when Belinda and I went into the bathroom together earlier, I told her that if any of the men asked her about tonight she had to tell them my parents were coming here.'

'Why for God's sake?'

'Because I thought she was the only one they would question.'

'Does Sarah know what you told Belinda to say?'

'No.'

'Has anyone questioned you Belinda?' Garroway said, turning to his daughter.

'Yes, the other one, Mr. Lorrimar, he asked

me when we were downstairs and I told him what Mother said I had to say.' Garroway nodded slowly and turned back to his wife.

'I think that will have alerted him that there is something they don't know about.'

'I think he had guessed that already. He knows something is wrong and I think the other man, the fat one, knows more than he has told the others.

'That still doesn't account for him . . .' he broke off as Hart came back into the room and closed the door.

'Plotting?' he asked casually as he dropped into a chair. 'Don't try it. It won't work, whatever it is.' Garroway had opened his mouth to reply when the bedroom door was suddenly banged open and Hart came to his feet, the heavy Smith & Wesson appearing in his hand. It was Mannion, his face was red and his eyes glittered angrily.

'Where's Lorrimar and the girl?' he snarled at Hart. The tall man relaxed without letting the barrel of the gun waver from alignment with Mannion's stomach.

'Outside,' he said. Garroway looked at his wife, his eyes trying to calm the panic he saw reappearing there.

'Why?' Mannion demanded. 'What's he up to?'

'Maybe he's telling her the story of his life,' Hart said languidly.

'What are you and Lorrimar trying?' Mannion asked, his eyes on the gun in Hart's hand.

'Why should we be trying anything Ken? We're all in this together, aren't we?' There was a moment of tense silence.

'What do you mean?' Mannion said eventually.

'Nothing Ken. Not a thing.'

'Listen . . .' Mannion started to speak again, his face reddening even more.

'Now let's all relax,' Hart said quietly. 'Dave's in charge of this little caper and if he wants to talk to the girl in private then I expect he's got a good reason for it.' Mannion looked at him angrily.

'I don't like it,' he said.

'Sit down, Ken,' Hart said. 'Sit down and calm down. When Dave gets back you can talk to him about it. Until then we're doing a job and that doesn't include sounding off at each other. Okay?' Mannion turned away and glared across the room at the Garroways. Then he did as Hart had said and sat down, glowering at the others, his colour slowly returning to normal. After several minutes Hart too sat down, but this time he didn't put away the Smith & Wesson. He let it rest along his thigh and neither the Garroways nor Mannion missed the significance of the change in his attitude.

In the shrubbery at the foot of the drive

Lorrimar waited quietly, unmoving in his crouched position. A few yards away, in the shrubbery at the opposite side of the drive, he heard Sarah Garroway constantly shifting her position. He carefully moved one hand so that he could see the luminous dial of his watch. They had been in the cold, damp bushes for over half an hour. Three cars had passed along the lane in that time and each time he had been aware that the woman had moved forward. He heard another car approaching and this time the engine note changed as it turned in and Lorrimar saw the woman clearly as she stepped out, her arms raised, to stop the car. The headlights held her for a moment then they were switched off. He eased himself to his feet and moved carefully towards the car, his movements made easier as the small noises were covered by the sound of the engine. He could see the girl, leaning forward and speaking to someone in the front passenger seat. As far as he could make out there were just two people in the car, the driver and the person the woman was speaking to. Then the rear door was opened to let the woman get in. Lorrimar heard the driver engage gear and the car started to edge slowly backwards. He stepped forward, reaching for the rear door, ready to change to the front door if it proved to be locked. It wasn't and he had opened the door and slid into the back seat beside Sarah Garroway before either of the two men in the front seats knew he was there.

'Okay,' he said. 'Fun and games over. Drive up to the house. No tricks. There's no need to turn round, the girl can tell you that I'm holding a gun. I can tell you it's a Smith & Wesson .44 and if it goes off it will take away most of her head. So let's do it my way. Right?' The only sound in the car was the murmur of the engine. Then the man in the passenger seat nodded his head and the driver carefully re-engaged gear and they moved slowly up the drive towards the Hall. The driver carefully manoeuvred around the Porsche and moments later they were on the level gravelled area in front of the Hall. 'Park beside the Rolls,' Lorrimar said. 'Now turn off the engine and drop the keys on the floor. The girl and I are getting out first, then you, driver, then you. And everybody does everything slowly.' He felt behind him and opened the door. Then he eased backwards out of the car. When the girl was out and standing by the door he tapped on the window by the driver. The door opened and the man climbed out and the second man followed. 'Very good. Very good,' Lorrimar said. 'Now everybody into the house, you two first and remember I'm right behind you and the gun is in the girl's back.' The small procession moved slowly up the steps and stopped. 'Open the door and push it right back. Take your hand off the door before you step through.' The driver did as Lorrimar instructed and the second man followed him. As Lorrimar and the girl stepped inside he kicked the door shut behind him. 'Down the hall,' he said. From upstairs they heard the sound of a door opening.

'Dave?'

'Okay Jim. Leave Ken up there and come down.' Moments later Hart came down the stairs and into the hall. He stopped, staring at the group facing him. His eyes moved from the driver to the second man and Lorrimar saw them widen in disbelief.

'Jesus Christ,' he said softly. 'Oh, Jesus bloody Christ.' Lorrimar stepped forward and reached out to grip the tall man by the shoulder. He spun him round and looked into his face. He felt his chest tighten and then he turned to Hart.

'Get Mannion,' he said savagely. 'Get the bastard down here.' Hart nodded and turned away. 'In the dining-room,' Lorrimar said and pushed the girl. She opened the door and went in, Lorrimar gestured with the Smith & Wesson and the two men followed. He heard footsteps on the stairs and moments later the rest of the Garroways came into the dining-room with Hart and a frightened-looking Mannion behind them. Lorrimar motioned to Hart to keep the group covered and then he stepped quickly towards Mannion. The fat man saw the expression in Lorrimar's eyes and his hand came up, the small revolver wavering. Lorrimar did not break step and he swept his own gun down, the barrel smashing onto Mannion's wrist. The revolver fell to the floor and Lorrimar scooped it up before pushing Mannion out into the hall. 'I'll get Bill,' he said over his shoulder to Hart. 'Then we're going to find out what this bastard is playing at.'

CHAPTER ELEVEN

Detective Chief Superintendent Arthur Mason had reached the office door when the telephone started to ring. He opened the door and thought very seriously about ignoring the summons. Then he sighed, closed the door and walked back to his desk. He picked up the instrument and grunted into it.

'Arthur?' He recognised the voice of one of his colleagues.

'Yes Ted.'

'Still there then.'

'I wouldn't have been if you had waited another minute before calling me. What is it?'

'Not sure Arthur, but it needs looking into right away. Maybe something, maybe nothing. Who can tell?'

'Oh, for Christ's sake Ted, get on with it.'

'Eh? Oh, sorry. We've had a call from a man named Stanley Klein. He's a big noise in the city. Works for the Garroway group. That's hardly the right word for what he does, he's a very big wheel indeed. Managing Director of three of the companies in the group, director of a few others and he's on the board of the holding company as well. Director responsible for finance.'

'Okay I'm impressed. Am I supposed to be?'

'I'm telling you that because what he called about would sound much less likely if it had come from the firm's office boy.'

'Go on.'

'He thinks Sir James Garroway is in some kind of trouble.'

'What kind of trouble?'

'He doesn't know and that's why he's talking to us.'

'Tell me.'

'Garroway telephoned Klein earlier this evening. He gave him certain instructions. These included preparing to liquidate certain of the group's assets. The liquidation has to be carried out with great speed so that the cash will be available on Monday.'

'Maybe he wants to buy a new yacht.'

'Garroway isn't that type. He's very spartan in his way of life. Not spartan as you or I would understand the word, but he doesn't flash his wealth about. Anyway you can buy a hell of a lot of yachts for four million pounds.'

'Four million?'

'Four million. That's what Garroway wants. By Monday.'

'Can that kind of money be produced at such short notice?'

'Klein seems to think it can, with a lot of hard work by a lot of people over the next thirty-six hours.'

'Okay, I'll go along that this might seem unusual, but I don't see where we come in. Is what Garroway wants doing illegal?'

'No. Provided he gets the agreement of the board of the holding company, he can do it.'

'Has he got that agreement?'

'Not yet, but he's instructed Klein to set up a board meeting on Monday morning. He said he would say then what he's doing, and why, and seek their approval.'

'So where's the problem?'

'Up to that point Klein was worried, but not excessively so. He knows Garroway well and he knows that if some kind of deal had come up in a hurry this might be the best way to handle things. But it would have to be very special for Klein not to know anything about it.'

'Ted, are you sure you shouldn't be talking to the fraud boys?'

'No, I don't think it's their kind of deal. I haven't finished.'

'Okay what else is there?'

'After he had told Klein what he wanted financially, he went on to ask for two more things to be standing by for Monday.'

'What?'

'A helicopter and an aircraft.' Mason sat silently for a moment.

'Okay,' he said slowly. 'What does Klein think?'

'He thinks Garroway is under some kind of pressure to produce the money.'

'Pressure?'

'Not financial pressure. Klein has a finger right on the financial pulse of the whole operation. There is nothing happening anywhere in the group that would warrant Garroway trying to do a bunk with some cash, if that's what you were thinking.'

'It had crossed my mind. It seems it also crossed Klein's mind.

'Yes, he seems a pretty thorough fellow. He didn't like the thought, but he checked it even so.'

'And came up with nothing?'

'That's right.'

'So, we've got a wealthy financier liquidating four million pounds and requesting a helicopter and an aircraft all to be ready for him for some time on Monday. And no explanations given for any of it?'

'No.'

'You said Klein thinks he's under some kind of pressure. What kind of pressure does he think it is?'

'He thinks it might be a kidnapping.'

'Who?'

'Garroway has two daughters and one of them is only twelve.'

'This is England, Ted, not Italy.'

'It's only a matter of time before somebody starts that kind of caper here. There've been a few attempts in the past, the recent past.'

'I suppose you're right. Okay what have you done so far?' He listened as his colleague ran through his actions which amounted to little more than a preliminary check on the financial status of the company and the principals. When the other man had finished speaking Mason thought for a moment. 'Okay Ted,' he said eventually. 'I'll take it from here. Let me have your notes right away will you. Oh, and you might send a copy to the Collator. Ask him to give it top priority.' He replaced the receiver and stood up to take off his overcoat. He sat down again and dialled a number.

'Jackson. Come in will you. And on your way organise some coffee and some sandwiches. We might have a long night ahead of us.' He glanced at his watch, pressed the telephone rest down, released it again and dialled for an outside line. Then he dialled his home telephone number and explained to his long-suffering and usually patient wife that he wouldn't be home for at least several hours and that she should go to bed without waiting up for him. It turned out to be

111

one of the occasions when her patience was less in evidence than usual. He listened to the tirade with one part of his brain already establishing procedures for the new investigation. When he sensed that his wife had calmed down enough he said a few harmlessly pleasant words and hung up. Within seconds his mind had completely shut off his private life and by the time his assistant, Detective Inspector Alan Jackson, had arrived, with coffee, sandwiches, and a pained expression, Mason was beginning to experience his usual pre-case sensations. Excitement, eagerness and the ever-present worry that things might get worse.

CHAPTER TWELVE

The four men in the Landrover were cold and tired and three of them were also extremely vocal about their discomfort. The fourth man, Andrew Webb, did not join in the general complaining. Not that he did not agree, he did, but as the only commissioned officer he felt he had to maintain a stoical silence. He also felt that he should stop the other soldiers from carrying on the way they were but, unfortunately, he was not very good with men, at least not in small identifiable groups. He was far happier with a large, anonymous crowd, even a parade ground full of them did not alarm him, but three were far too intimate. It didn't help matters that all three were older than he was; the two riflemen were both two years older than his twenty four and the sergeant was forty three. Webb concentrated on his driving, hoping that the others would assume his silence was due simply to that concentration, for, apart from feeling he should order them to be quiet, he also felt he should try to be one of them. Life, in or out of the modern British Army, was not easy for him.

The four men had been engaged in week-long manoeuvres that almost nobody understood, although all had accepted them gratefully as a break from routine. They had come up from Salisbury Plain the previous Sunday and had followed a series of complex instructions for the next six days. Now, under orders to return, they had suffered the indignity of two punctures within the space of an hour and had had to stop to carry out running repairs. The rest of the convoy was now several miles ahead of them and that much closer to fires and hot drinks and sleep.

'Do you think we should take a break and have something to eat sir?' The quiet, blurred Mid-Lothian accent of Sergeant Kenneth McIntosh was deceptive, as Webb knew. When roused, which was often, McIntosh could devastate anyone within earshot, and within earshot meant anyone up to a quarter of a mile away. Webb thought about the request. He could see no reason for not granting it, in fact the only thing about it that he didn't like was that he hadn't thought of it himself.

'Yes, righto Sergeant. It's getting late, we'd better stop at the next café we see.'

'I was thinking more of a pub sir,' McIntosh said quietly. Webb worried over that. After a moment he thought of a compromise.

'Whichever we see first Sergeant,' he said. McIntosh leaned back, clearly well-satisfied. Statistically he felt certain that a pub would appear long before they reached a café. In the centrally facing seats at the back of the Landrover, cramped and uncomfortable amongst a clutter of radio equipment, Riflemen Ian Lowe and Harry Manning grinned at one another. Unable themselves to manipulate the young lieutenant, they gained consoling satisfaction from seeing the stockily-built, ginger haired sergeant in action. Five minutes later McIntosh's statistical guess was proved correct as they saw the illuminated sign of a pub. The saloon bar was already crowded and McIntosh took the orders and fought his way to the bar. He took drinks back to Webb and Manning and then took a pint of bitter out to Lowe, who, having lost the toss of a coin, was still sitting in the Landrover. That had been at Lieutenant Webb's insistence and none of the others had been able to disagree, not that the Landrover and the radio equipment were in much danger of theft, but their four SLR's, Webb's nine millimetre Browning semi-automatic pistol and several boxes of ammunition would have attracted the attention of any passing villain.

Back inside the pub McIntosh collected a small mountain of sandwiches the landlord had produced and after filling a tray with another round of drinks he made his way to the corner where Webb and Manning had found room to stand.

'Lowe okay?' Webb asked the sergeant.

'He's fine sir. Here, Harry, take him something to eat,' McIntosh said to Manning. The tall, fair-haired private swallowed the rest of his first pint of beer and took a handful of sandwiches and another pint glass and shouldered his way through the regulars.

'Let's not make a night of it Mac,' Webb said, allowing himself the luxury of informality.

'No fear of that,' McIntosh said. 'Anyway it's past ten now, I expect they close at half-past.' Webb nodded his head and McIntosh grinned into his second pint, hiding the knowledge that the pub wouldn't close until eleven which gave him a chance to replace some of the liquid he had sweated out during the preceding six days. After all, that late on a Saturday night they were as well off in a pub in Nettlebed as they would have been out on the road heading for Salisbury Plain.

Less than five miles away from Nettlebed, by road, the Fenton Oak was even more crowded and Simon Arne and his regular barmen, together with the Saturday night extra help, were beginning to feel the effects of three hours uninterrupted activity.

'Where the hell are they all coming from?' Peter, Arne's right hand man, complained.

'All in a day's work,' Arne murmured.

'Some day. I haven't seen this many since last summer. Must be a bad night on the telly.' He darted off to replace an empty bottle on one of the optics behind the bar. Arne glanced at his watch and opened the door of the office and looked in.

'Hello, Mr. Blake,' he said to the police constable. 'Be with you in a minute.' He served two more customers and then seeing that Peter was once more in full control he poured a single whisky and went into the office.

'Busy,' the policeman remarked. 'Haven't seen that many cars in the car park since the summer.'

'No, Peter was just saying it must be a bad night on the telly.'

'Locals?'

'There are quite a number from Henley. I recognised half a dozen from one of the rugby clubs.'

116

'Likely to give you any bother?'

'I shouldn't think so. Apart from a few unrepeatable songs and stories they're usually fairly harmless.' Blake nodded and finished his drink.

'Well don't let me keep you.' He handed Arne the price of the drink. 'I might come back through this way, later on. About half past eleven.'

'Fine. Will you call in?'

'No, you'll want to be getting locked up by then I expect.' Arne nodded and smiled at the slightly tactless way the policeman had worded his warning, aware that it was meant in his best interests. Blake went out of the door and paused in the passage to glance into the bar. Then he went out of the front door of the inn and climbed into his Landrover. He drove up the road past the church and turned into Remenham Lane and headed for the eastern extremity of his beat. He reckoned that there and back would be just about right to bring him to the Oak for eleven-thirty.

CHAPTER THIRTEEN

When the telephone on Mason's desk rang, he motioned to Detective Inspector Jackson to take the call.

'Detective Chief Superintendent Mason's office, Detective Inspector Jackson speaking,' he announced, taking a perverse satisfaction in annoying the caller with the long introduction. He listened for a moment. 'Hold on,' he said abruptly, interested for the first time since Mason had called him into the office. 'It's the Collator,' he said, 'you'd better come on the line sir, first time I've heard the bugger get excited since he's been here.' The Collator was a slightly built, fleshless man, with washed out blue eyes and a pale prison-like pallor that seldom saw the light of day. He had spent most of his police service flitting from one record department to another until finally finding his true vocation when he had been appointed as Collator to the Serious Crimes Division at New Scotland Yard, where his passion for facts, allied with a phenomenal memory, had made him more use than any of his superior officers liked to admit. His name was Maxwell and he was known to everyone as Max the Facts. Mason picked up the extension and pressed the button that let him onto the line without disconnecting

Jackson.

'What is it Max?'

'You had a copy of a report sent in. Concerning Sir James Garroway.' He had a dry papery voice that sounded like the pages of one of his files being turned.

'Yes,' Mason said.

'He lives at Fenton Hall, Fenton. Fenton is a village on the Oxfordshire–Buckinghamshire border. Not all that far from Henley.'

'Yes,' Mason said patiently, knowing from bitter experience that Maxwell would not be hurried.

'We had a report through last week, no connection other than it also involved Fenton village.'

'In what way?'

'The local bobby asked for a check on a man staying at the village pub, a place called the Fenton Oak. The man was Dave Lorrimar.'

'Lorrimar?'

'Yes. He was using his own name, somebody looked into it and made a few enquiries.' Mason became aware that Jackson's face was turning bright red. 'An Inspector called Jackson,' Maxwell went on, remorselessly.

'Okay Max. Thanks,' Mason said. 'Keep a tight eye on this will you, anything else that looks interesting get straight on to me. Could be a big one.' He replaced the receiver and looked at Jackson with a not entirely unkindly eye.

'Well?' he asked.

'Sorry sir. Forgot it completely. I didn't associate the Fenton Oak with Fenton Hall.'

'Well, never mind, that's what we pay Maxwell for. Tell me about it.'

'As he said, the local man reported in, he said there was nothing to justify it, he simply felt that the man looked as if he might be a villain. He gave us a description, the name the man was using and the number of the car. Our people checked it all out and it was Lorrimar. As he was using his own name we didn't think anything of it. I checked up on the girl he had with him. She was booked at the pub as his wife. It was Linda Hooper, one of the girls from the Longboat.'

'That all?'

'All I can remember sir. Maybe I'd better get the file.'

'Yes do that. The village copper. Fairly bright lad?'

'Seems so.'

'Maybe we'd better use him then.'

'Use him?'

'Yes, if there is something going on at the Hall, if Stanley Klein is right, then we don't want to go riding in there like the U.S. Cavalry do we?'

'No sir.'

'Right, get the file and while we're at it we'd better have Lorrimar's and also get onto West

120

End Central. Look out for him and report in if they see him. Also ... no, you do that for a start, I'll make some calls myself.' Jackson crossed to the door and hesitated.

'Are we taking this kidnapping theory seriously sir?'

'Not necessarily but there's one area where Max the Facts and I agree. We both like coincidences. He likes 'em because it gives him a reason for living. I like 'em because I don't believe in 'em. And nine times out of ten I'm right for not believing. Go on, get moving lad.' After Jackson had gone hurrying down the corridor Mason leaned back in his chair and thought for a few minutes, then he pulled the telephone towards him and dialled.

'Ted, it's me, Arthur. Your friend Mr. Klein. Get him in will you. Fastish.'

'What's happened?'

'Nothing yet, but if I had a corn it would be starting to twitch.'

'Right, need any more men?'

'Yes, for now let's have a full incident centre set-up prepared.'

'Where?'

'Not sure yet, but let's be ready.' He replaced the receiver and scratched his head. He picked up his coffee cup and drank, grimaced and stood up to open the door. He saw a young constable sitting laboriously typing with two fingers. 'You lad, organise some coffee will you, a lot of it.

121

Then drop what you're doing and help Inspector Jackson.' He closed the door and stood rubbing his hands together. He was beginning to enjoy himself.

An hour later the enjoyment had not waned, although to the majority of the men in the room with him he appeared to be edgily irritable with everything and everybody. The room was crowded, apart from Mason there was Inspector Jackson, the constable snatched from an evening of typing reports, Detective Chief Superintendent Ted Armstrong, three sergeants and four constables rescued from what they had all hoped was to be an early night, and Stanley Klein. Klein had just completed his fourth account of Sir James Garroway's telephone call. The first account had been when he had telephoned Ted Armstrong, the second was when he repeated it in writing, the third was when he told the story to Mason and now, for the fourth time, to the room full of detectives. He didn't object. The concern with which the Serious Crimes Division were treating his hastily formed opinion, impressed him. It also perturbed him a little and he had said as much to Mason; he was concerned that he might be wasting everyone's time. Mason had convinced him that there was no need for worry on that particular count, that everyone would be pleased if it turned out to be a false alarm but implying that already, with very little to go on,

122

the police were beginning to think his way. After the fourth account Mason asked Klein to return to his office, going home would put him too far out of touch, and with him he sent a detective sergeant with certain specific instructions. Now Mason called for comments on the story Klein had told after first adding the information supplied by the Collator.

'It sounds like Garroway is pulling some big deal in the city,' one detective volunteered, hoping everyone would agree with him so that he could get home before the late-night movie started.

'Either that or he's ready to do a bunk,' another suggested. 'Shouldn't we ask the Frauds and Fiddles lads to look at it on Monday?'

'According to Klein there is nothing wrong with the company,' Jackson put in.

'Would he know?' the first man asked, becoming interested despite himself. 'If Garroway is on the fiddle then maybe he's getting out now, before Klein gets wind of it.'

'Then why involve Klein in the cash raising side of things? If he was on the run the only thing he'd do with Klein is send him on a long holiday.' There was silence in the room, then one of the constables coughed and looked slightly embarrassed. Mason looked at him encouragingly.

'I take it we're keeping away from the house

where Garroway is, in case Klein is right?'

'Yes.'

'Isn't that putting Garroway and maybe his family at risk?'

'No, if he is under duress then he wouldn't appear to be in any immediate danger. After all they're letting him come to his office on Monday.'

'I think we ought to try to have a look at them sir,' the constable persisted doggedly.

'We will,' Mason said. 'Tomorrow, we'll get the local man to pay a visit.'

'Until then we do nothing?' One or two of the men brightened as their early night looked a little more likely.

'Not exactly,' Mason said, destroying their hopes. 'I want a full check on Lorrimar and his known associates. You,' he pointed at one of the remaining sergeants, 'take two men and have a look at Lorrimar's flat.'

'Search warrant?'

'What do you think?' The sergeant grinned.

'Right sir.' Mason turned to the second sergeant.

'You take two men and stand by for reports on Lorrimar's associates of the past few weeks. As they come in do the same, a quick check on their homes. Anything you turn up, radio straight in. That goes for all of you, don't mess about with written reports, we want information and we want it fast. Okay?' The men nodded and mumbled assent and gradually shuffled out of the room. When they had gone there was only Ted Armstrong and the one remaining constable. 'You, lad, what's your name?'

'Mather sir.'

'You stay by the telephone. Extra lines are coming in.' He glanced at the other Chief Superintendent for confirmation and Armstrong nodded his head. 'We're also putting a tap on the line into Klein's office. As soon as it's installed Klein will be calling Garroway, ostensibly to give him a progress report on what he's doing about raising the money. It'll give us a chance to hear what Garroway sounds like. Mind you, Klein said he sounded normal and he should know.' The constable went out of the room and Mason looked at his colleague.

'Well Ted?'

'Well?'

'What do you think?'

'Not sure, inclining towards believing that Klein is right.'

'So am I, only more so. I'm bloody sure he's right. Mind you it bothers me that Dave Lorrimar's involved.'

'Why?'

'It's not his style. Bank robbery, yes. Bullion snatches, yes. Any big-time heavy operation, yes. But kidnapping. Doesn't seem to fit.'

'There's four million reasons for him to change his style.'

'I expect so.' Mason leaned forward and picked up a copy of the statement Stanley Klein had made. 'Notice anything about the other things they asked for?'

'The helicopter and the aircraft?'

'Yes.'

'What about them?'

'They asked. for ... sorry, Garroway has asked for a helicopter to be lined up for him. He hasn't said where he wants it yet, but he wants one. Same with the aeroplane.'

'So?'

'The helicopter is just that. A helicopter, no type, no description, nothing. Just that it can carry seven people apart from the pilot.'

'Yes?'

'Come on Ted, you took the statement down and you've heard him repeat it twice more.' Mason grinned at his colleague. 'The aircraft is also a seven-seater plus the pilot, but there Garroway wasn't so vague. He didn't just say, an aircraft, the way he just said, a helicopter. He has specifically asked for a Cessna Citation 500.'

'Meaning?'

'Meaning? I don't know. But there has to be a reason for everything, hasn't there?' He clambered heavily to his feet and looked around the office. 'Christ, why are policemen such untidy buggers?' He opened the office door and peered out at the constable sitting before a bank of telephones. 'Get some more coffee will you lad.' He closed the door and sank back into his chair.

'Are we really going to sit here until Monday with only a visit up to the Garroway house by the village copper between now and then?' Armstrong said.

'Why, beginning to feel more certain?' Armstrong grinned.

'I think I am,' he said. 'Well, are we going to sit here doing nothing?'

'No, maybe not. What was that lad's name again?' Mason jerked his thumb at the wall separating him from the young constable.

'Mather.'

'Mather,' Mason yelled. The constable appeared at the door looking nervous.

'Yes sir.'

'Talk to Thames Valley. I want to know how to make contact with the village bobby. His name's . . .' he looked at Armstrong.

'Blake,' the other man supplied.

'Yes sir. Do you want me to raise him or just find out how he can be contacted?'

'For now just ask where he makes his stops. Then get telephone numbers. No special radio contact to be made.' The constable disappeared.

'We'd better have a word with Thames Valley, Arthur. They won't like us treading on their patch without a word of explanation, to say nothing of getting their Chief's permission,' Armstrong said.

127

'No I suppose not. Will you do that Ted?'

'Yes, okay.' Armstrong went out of the room and Mason sat staring at his desk for a moment. He gathered together the various pieces of paper he had been scribbling on and glanced over them. Then he reached for the telephone.

'Mather,' he said when the constable answered. 'Have a word with Chief Inspector Kelly at Cannon Row. Ask him the name of the flying school where Jim Hart learned to fly.'

'Jim Hart?'

'Yes, he'll know who you mean.' He replaced the receiver and smiled at the littered office. He liked few things better than being one jump ahead of his men, even if the jump was made by guesswork and not by deduction. In fact he usually preferred it when the advantage was gained by guesswork. It gave the men something to worry over.

CHAPTER FOURTEEN

It was a few minutes after eleven before reports began to trickle in from the men assigned by Mason to the Garroway case. The tap was on Klein's telephone and a tape recording of the finance director of the Garroway group's conversation with Sir James had been made. The sergeant who had made the recording told

Mason that Garroway had sounded calm and unflustered and Klein had also confirmed that there was nothing in the financier's voice that indicated he was under any form of duress. Klein sounded apologetic but Mason was unperturbed. He learned, from Kelly, that Hart had learned his flying at Blackbushe Flying School. He contacted the senior flying instructor and had it confirmed that the biggest aircraft Hart had flown, and the one on which he had most flying hours, was a Cessna Citation 500. He instructed an immediate turn-over of Hart's flat and was pleased to hear the surprise in the sergeant's voice. The man had been on the point of calling in to say that Hart and Lorrimar had been seen in each other's company during the preceding few weeks and he had been about to announce that he planned to visit Hart's flat next. The sergeant climbed back into his car muttering about Chief Superintendents who kept things to themselves.

Mason was finishing off his fourteenth cup of coffee when Armstrong came into the room.

'Thames Valley are cleared. I've spoken to the Assistant Chief. He's okayed it.'

'Where was the head lad? Not working late like the rest of us poor sods?' Mason asked amiably.

'No, he's out at some soup, fish and foxtrot do at Reading.'

'Where would we be without our Chief

Constables?' Mason sighed.

'Exactly where we are now,' Armstrong said. The telephone on Mason's desk rang and he picked it up.

'Yes.' He listened for a few moments. 'Okay,' he said. 'Follow it up and see where it leads.' He replaced the receiver and looked at Armstrong. 'That was Jackson. He's talked to the woman Lorrimar took to the pub at Fenton. Seems he spent most of the time walking around the village. She didn't go with him, but she got the impression he was looking at the place very carefully. She thought he was planning to buy a house there.'

'Not very likely.'

'No. She also said that he's been seeing Kenneth Mannion recently.'

'Has he now. That means something big. Mannion doesn't get involved in peanut cases.'

'Jackson's going round to see Mannion.'

'He's still in town then?'

'I expect so. He doesn't dirty his hands so he'll be where everybody can see him and give him a big fat alibi.'

'So, we've got Mannion for planning, Lorrimar for running the show, Hart the mechanic. If it's what we think it is, there'll be at least two others, maybe more.'

'Likely.'

'So the pieces are starting to fit.'

'Seems like it. I think we should have a word

with that copper out there. Mather.' The last word was shouted out again and the constable appeared at the door of the office almost instantly.

'Yes sir.'

'Got the movements for the man on the beat at Fenton?'

'Yes sir.' Mather disappeared again and returned seconds later with a sheet of paper in his hand. 'His last call where he can be reached by telephone was at the Fenton Oak at about ten-thirty. After that he can only be reached by radio until he gets back to the police house at about midnight.'

'Okay, ring the house, I take it he's got a wife there?'

'Yes sir.'

'Give her this number. He's to call in immediately he gets home.'

'Yes sir.' Mather closed the door and Mason leaned back in his chair.

'Well Ted, I think we'll wait until this lad 'phones in and then, unless he has anything startling to tell us, we'll call it a night.'

'Sure?'

'You mean, am I sure that's the way to play it? No I'm not, but until we have something concrete I don't think we can risk anything more positive.'

'I expect you're right. Okay we wait for Constable Blake. I wonder what the lad would think if he knew half the Serious Crimes squad was hanging on his next words.'

'Either frighten him silly or make him start thinking about his first promotion.' Mason grinned at Armstrong. 'Christ, Ted,' he went on, 'how many years is it since you and me were coppers on the beat?'

'Too bloody many by far,' Armstrong said.

★   ★   ★

For the object of their thoughts, it had proved to be an entirely uneventful evening. Police Constable Raymond Blake had patrolled to the edge of his beat and was driving leisurely back towards Fenton. He turned out of Remenham Lane and into the road that led towards the village centre. As he passed the driveway to the Hall he glanced to his right and he caught a slight glimmer of reflected light. He slowed the Landrover and thought about stopping and then thought not and then thought again and stopped. By that time he was over a hundred yards past the drive but instead of reversing he climbed out and walked back. He turned into the drive and walked a few yards along the gravel until he saw the outline of a car. Close to, he recognised it as Sarah Garroway's Porsche. He shone the torch into it and then looked up towards the Hall.

'Probably broke down,' he murmured to

himself. He thought about going up to the Hall, but there were no lights visible at the front of the big house. He turned and walked back to his Landrover and climbed in and drove down towards the Oak. As he approached the inn he was surprised to see the door open and Simon Arne come out and wave to him. He stopped the Landrover, climbed out and walked across to the older man.

'Hello Mr. Blake, glad I saw you,' Arne said.

'Trouble Mr. Arne?'

'Trouble? Oh, no, not here. Your wife called a few minutes ago. Seems she's had a call for you. Someone wants you to call them as soon as you get back home. She thinks it's rather important and she decided to try to get hold of you sooner than that.'

'I'd better get off then, I was on my way.'

'Call her from here. She might be right, it might be important.' Arne turned away and pushed open the door.

'Thank you,' Blake said, following Arne into the hallway. The two men went down to the office.

'I'll leave you to it,' Arne said and went through into the bar. Blake picked up the telephone and called his home number. He listened to what his wife said and then called out to Arne.

'Do you mind if I make a call, long distance?' Arne opened the door.

'Of course not, go ahead.'

'I'll pay for it,' the policeman said and Arne grinned.

'We'll not argue over that,' he said. The police constable was speaking to Detective Chief Superintendent Mason within seconds of the call being answered by the Yard's switchboard. He told Mason who he was.

'Ah, Blake. Good man,' Mason said blandly. 'That report of yours the other day about David Lorrimar, one of our local bad lads, good thinking that, we can do with a few more alert young constables around.'

'Thank you sir,' Blake said, wondering why a senior officer from the Yard had chosen to put out an urgent message to him late on a Saturday night.

'Tell me,' Mason went on, 'anything else happened around your way since then?'

'What kind of thing sir? I've seen no one else like Lorrimar if that's what you mean.'

'No. I mean anything at all.' Mason said, deliberately avoiding mention of Garroway. Blake thought for a moment. Then he decided on an admission that might cause loss of face, but would ease matters with the Yard man.

'As a matter of fact it was Mr. Arne who pointed Lorrimar out to me. He's the owner of the pub here. That's where I'm speaking from now. He thought Lorrimar seemed a bit out of place here. I can ask him if he's seen anything.'

134

'Do that,' Mason said. Blake rested the telephone on the top of Arne's desk and walked across to the door.

'Mr. Arne. You remember that fellow we talked about, Lorrimar?'

'Yes.'

'You haven't seen anything of him or anything else that might be of interest?'

'No, nothing. Wait a minute though. This morning, there was a car like his up at the Hall. But I don't suppose for a moment it was the same one. They're not uncommon and I hardly think he would be a friend of Sir James'.' Blake thought for a moment, he remembered the unoccupied Porsche in the drive and that, added to the fact that the Scotland Yard officer thought it necessary to call him, took on a new meaning. He walked back to the telephone.

'Sir?'

'Yes.'

'Er, is there anything happening that involves Sir James Garroway?' There was a pause while Mason signalled to Ted Armstrong to pick up another telephone. Blake heard the other instrument click into the line.

'Okay Blake,' Mason said. 'Go ahead.' Succinctly Blake told the Chief Superintendent about the two cars. When he had finished there was a long silence before Mason spoke again.

'Right Blake. This is what you do. Stay exactly where you are. Tell the owner of the place, Mr . . .'

'Arne.'

'Tell Mr Arne we're setting up an incident centre on his premises. If he complains tell him . . .'

'He won't sir,' Blake interrupted.

'Fine. Can you see the Hall from where you are?'

'No sir, wait a moment though.' Blake turned to find Arne standing at the open doorway. 'Where were you when you saw the car at the Hall?'

'In one of the bedrooms.'

'Is the room occupied now?'

'Yes.'

'Can it be seen from any other room?'

'No.'

'Are you there sir? The Hall can be seen from one of the bedrooms and nowhere else in the place. The room's occupied, do you want me to have the occupier of the room moved?'

'No, not yet. We'll decide that when we get there.'

'Yes sir.'

'Now listen carefully Blake. In no circumstances are you to go up to the Hall. Stay where you are and stay near the telephone. You're about due to go off duty I understand?'

'Yes sir.'

'Well, telephone your wife and tell her you're going to be late. Then radio in as if you're going off watch in the usual way, that's just in case anyone is listening in to the police waveband. Then get your vehicle out of sight. After that stay near that telephone. If anything happens call this number and you'll be connected to me in my car. Give me your number.'

'Fenton four-nine-one.'

'Remember, don't use your radio, use the telephone.'

'Yes sir.'

'We'll be with you in about an hour. All clear?'

'Yes sir.' The telephone went dead and Blake replaced the instrument carefully. He looked up at Arne. The older man was looking at him with unconcealed curiosity. 'Well,' Blake said. 'I don't know what this is all about but it's something big.' He smiled uncertainly at Arne. 'I'm afraid you've been commandeered Mr. Arne,' he added.

'Commandeered?'

'The Oak is to be used as an incident centre as soon as they all get here.'

'They?'

'The Serious Crimes Division from the Yard.' Arne frowned.

'Something connected with the Hall?'

'Seems so. Look I have to get my Landrover out of sight. I'll move it into your car park.'

'If you want it hidden there's my garage. I'll bring my car out into the yard.'

'That might be best.' The two men walked out of the office. Arne went down the passage into the car park and Blake went out of the front door and drove the Landrover around to the back of the inn. He called into his radio headquarters and signed himself off watch, then he drove the Landrover into the garage vacated by Arne. The two men walked back across the car park and had just reached the door of the inn when Arne stopped the younger man.

'Listen,' he said. They stood in silence. Then Blake heard it too.

'Aircraft?'

'No,' Arne said. 'Helicopters, two of them by the sound of it. And they're coming close.' He opened the door and went down the hall of the Oak and out again through the front door. 'There.' He pointed as two beams of light struck down out of the sky.

'They're landing,' Blake said.

'Yes. By the look of it they're coming down in the field beyond the churchyard.'

'I'd better take a look,' Blake said. Arne reached out and gripped his arm.

'Is that what you were told to do?' Blake looked at him.

'No, the Chief Superintendent said I had to stay where I was, but he wasn't talking about helicopters. It'll be the army on a night exercise or something. If there is something going on at the Hall, we want them to stay well clear.'

'I think you should talk to your superiors first Raymond,' Arne said. Blake looked at him in surprise at the use of his first name. Then he shook his head.

'No,' he said. 'I know you mean well Mr. Arne, but I think I'd better have a look first.' He turned away and hurried quietly up the road towards the church. Arne shook his head in annoyance, then he turned and went inside to the office. Near the telephone he saw the number the policeman had called. He stood for a moment looking down at it. Then, abruptly reaching a decision, he went up the stairs and into his own bedroom. From a cupboard he took an under and over shot gun. He slipped on a heavy anorak and filled the pockets with shells. Then, with the shot gun under his arm, he went back down the stairs and, after locking the door of the Oak behind him, he followed Police Constable Blake up the village street.

CHAPTER FIFTEEN

Second Lieutenant Andrew Webb was angry. Angry with his men and angry with himself. He was angry with the men because they had silently bullied him into staying longer at the Nettlebed pub than he had wanted to and he was angry with himself for allowing himself to be bullied. Not that anything had been said or done, it hadn't, but Sergeant McIntosh's methods were difficult for an inexperienced officer to combat. McIntosh had very soon surrounded himself with a cluster of men in the corner of the bar. All older men, and all with one kind of war service or another, they had taken to the hard-talking, hard-drinking and obviously hard-fighting sergeant. Webb had been gradually edged out of the conversation as he realised that he knew so little about the realities of war. His one short tour of Northern Ireland paled into insignificance beside McIntosh's three Northern Ireland tours, a spell in Cyprus during their troubles, the brief, abortive Suez campaign and long and arduous campaigns in Korea and Malaya.

The ex-army men had talked on, long after closing time, which had turned out to be at eleven o'clock, not the ten-thirty Webb had expected. When they finally stood outside, in the cold air, preparing to climb back into the Landrover it was almost midnight. Then, as they settled themselves in the vehicle, Rifleman Lowe decided that his long period of waiting in the cold had to be relieved by a visit to the lavatory. The landlord had hastily locked up and the soldier had to content himself with going around the back of the already darkened building. Webb switched off the engine and they waited in an irritable silence. All three men

140

heard the helicopters at the same time. McIntosh slid open the window and looked out, twisting his head so that he could peer upwards. He pulled his head back inside and looked at Webb.

'Funny,' he said.

'What?' Webb asked, still fuming.

'No lights on them. Two of them and flying in close formation.'

'No lights?'

'No.'

'I expect there's a reason sergeant.'

'I expect there is sir, and the best reason is that they don't want anyone to see them.'

'With the noise they are making sergeant, I imagine everybody in the neighbourhood knows they are there.'

'Maybe sir, but...' He was interrupted as Lowe returned to the vehicle.

'See them sarge?' he said as he clambered into the back of the Landrover.

'Yes. Where were they headed?'

'East, near enough. And losing height.'

'Shall we be moving on?' Webb asked, attempting to inject sarcasm into his voice.

'Losing height?' McIntosh said, ignoring the officer.

'Yes,' Lowe confirmed.

'Sergeant...' Webb began.

'Seems odd doesn't it sir?' McIntosh asked. 'Maybe we should have a look.'

'Oh for . . .' Webb hesitated and remembered something he had been told by one of the non-commissioned officer instructors at Sandhurst. He tried to think of the exact words, 'never ignore the instincts of a man who has faced death more times than you have yourself.' He looked at the sergeant, there were no signs that the man had consumed several pints of beer and at least three whiskies. He wondered if the instructor had allowed for the effect of a large intake of alcohol on the instincts of the man he had referred to in his remarks. Then, abruptly, he made up his mind.

'Have a look at the map Lowe,' he said. He leaned forward and switched on the engine, engaged gear and they shot out of the car park, spraying gravel, as he built up speed. He worked out some of his frustrations by bringing the Landrover up to high speed in the shortest possible time. Before Rifleman Lowe had located their position on the map they were already two miles along the road leading back towards Henley-on-Thames. The rifleman leaned forward and passed the map to McIntosh.

'About there,' he said. McIntosh looked at the place where Lowe's finger pointed, he took the map, holding it up in the glow of the interior light.

'Right,' he said. 'Straight down here sir, place called Lower Assendon. There'll be a left turn just as we reach it, go down there and we start keeping our eyes open.' Webb nodded in the darkness that descended as the sergeant switched off the light.

It took them little more than five minutes to reach the turning McIntosh had described. They turned into the road and the headlights picked out a roadsign.

'Fenton, Stonor and Fawley,' McIntosh announced. He flicked on the interior light and checked the map. 'If they did come down they could be anywhere along here.' Webb slowed the Landrover and then stopped. He turned off the engine.

'Listen,' he said. The four men sat in silence. 'Nothing,' he said.

'No, that means they've come down.'

'Or gone flying off somewhere else,' Webb said.

'Don't think so sir.'

'Where does that road go?' Webb asked, pointing ahead to a signpost a few yards ahead. McIntosh looked at the map again.

'Leads to Remenham,' he said. Webb grunted.

'Okay,' he said. 'We'll drive down the road to the first village. If we see nothing we turn back.' McIntosh looked at him.

'Yes sir,' he said. He reached into the back of the vehicle and picked up his SLR. Manning and Lowe, taking their cue from McIntosh picked up their rifles too. Webb sat undecided, then he turned.

'Right Lowe, you come up here and drive. You stay where you are sergeant, I'll get in the back with Manning.' He opened the door and climbed out as Lowe began to scramble forward into the driver's seat. Webb walked round to the back of the Landrover, he started to climb in and then caught his hand on the remaining SLR. He had picked it up, to move it further into the vehicle, when the firing started. He heard it as if it was coming from another world. The sustained fire was unlike anything he had heard during his Northern Ireland tour and he had almost discounted the evidence of his own ears when he felt the Landrover rock with the impact of the bullets. He heard the shattering of glass and then the screaming from the front of the vehicle. Instinctively he turned and dived for the roadside. Behind him he heard Manning scramble from the vehicle and follow. The rifleman fell across Webb as the two men hugged the ground. Then, suddenly, there was light from the Landrover and looking up Webb realised it was on fire. He had started to rise to his feet when Manning caught at him and pulled him backwards and the two men rolled over and down into a ditch at the roadside.

'You fool,' Webb yelled. 'We have to get . . .' The rest of his words were lost as the Landrover's petrol tank exploded with a

144

shattering roar. All at once Second Lieutenant Webb began to act like a soldier. He pulled Manning's head close to his and yelled into his ear. 'Back, down the ditch. Look for a way through into the field on the right.' With the rifleman leading they scrambled and slid along the ditch. Water and mud up to their knees made progress difficult, then Manning moved off to the right. Webb followed and they were in another ditch running at right-angles to the first. Fifty yards along the second ditch Webb reached out and caught Manning's foot. 'Wait,' he said softly. He stood up and looked cautiously over the top of the ditch. 'Right,' he whispered when he had rejoined Manning. 'We stay in the ditch for another twenty yards, then we go out on this side and make off to the left. There's a row of trees. Once we are in there we can have another look around and see where the enemy position is. With luck we might be behind them and can move in from their rear.'

'Enemy?' Manning said.

'What else would you call them?' Webb started to move along the ditch but Manning stopped him.

'Are you going to attack them sir?'

'I'm going to find out what we're up against and then I shall either attack them or go for help.' He started to move again, and again the rifleman hesitated.

'Sir,' he said.

'What is it?'

'I haven't got my rifle sir.' Webb swore silently to himself.

'Right,' he said. 'When we get up into the woods you can stay there while I have a closer look.' He moved off down the ditch and after the barest hesitation Manning followed.

CHAPTER SIXTEEN

Police Constable Raymond Blake was a few yards from the churchyard when he heard the sound of voices. They seemed to come from his left and he stopped and looked over the wall that bordered the garden of Home Farm. He saw that lights were on at the windows and he could see the Morgan family clustered at the windows looking towards the field adjoining the churchyard. Then he saw that the voices came from two men, standing in the garden close to the wall, with their backs to him. He moved forward and he opened his mouth to speak when he heard the sound of shots being fired. The sound came from some distance away, towards Lower Assendon. Blake turned and started to run back towards the Fenton Oak. Behind him he heard a harsh metallic sound and then a voice called out. He was aware that the language was not English, and then he heard the sound of shots again, only this time they were coming from close at hand. Absurdly he remembered he had not telephoned his wife to tell her he would be late home and then he felt a crashing blow in the middle of his back, a blow that flung him forward onto his face. He lay there on the ground listening to the footsteps that ran up to him. He didn't hear the next shot that was fired.

Simon Arne had also heard the distant sound of firing and he had instinctively fallen into the habits drilled into him over his many years in the army. He had dived into the cover offered by a hedge and he stayed there, motionless, while he assessed what was happening. He decided that the shots had been fired at a range of about half a mile and guessed at somewhere close to Fenton Hall Farm. Then he heard a sound from closer to hand and peering out of the hedge he saw the young police constable running towards him. The sudden burst of automatic firing seemed to come from the gardens of Home Farm and as Blake pitched forward onto his face, he saw two men clamber over the wall of the garden and run up to where the policeman lay. He saw one of the two men point his weapon at Blake's head and this time there was just one shot. Arne was gripped by a terrible rage, but his years of training held good. He knew that the shotgun he carried was no match for the fire-power of the two men, even if he had been lucky and hit them both with the two barrels, there were still the men who were firing at the other end of the village. He stayed where he was, face down in the grass to prevent reflected light. He heard the two men speak, but their voices were soft and he could not make out any words. The two men started to move at a gentle trot and they passed his position as they headed on down Fawley Road. After several moments Arne wriggled up into a crouching position. From the direction of Home Farm he could hear shouts and recognised the bull-like voice of old Sam Morgan. Arne looked in all directions, but could see nothing. He turned away and, still clinging to the hedge for cover, he went back to the Oak. He let himself in through the front door and hurried along to the office in the darkness. He propped the shotgun against the desk and fumbled in a drawer for a box of matches. He struck a match and cupping his hands around it, he checked the number Blake had written down. Then he blew out the match and dialled. The telephone was answered instantly.

'This is Simon Arne at the Fenton Oak,' he said.

'Yes Mr. Arne,' the voice that answered was young.

'You spoke to Police Constable Blake earlier?'

'That would be Chief Superintendent Mason,' the voice said.

'Whoever it was, there's trouble here, Blake

148

has . . .' Arne heard a creaking sound from the corridor and he carefully laid the telephone on the desk and reached for the shotgun. He stepped to the door and waited, behind him he could hear the tinny chatter as the man on the other end of the telephone tried to make himself heard. The office door opened slowly and Arne brought up the shotgun. Then a man stepped through, he was carrying a torch and in the faint backlight thrown up from the beam, Arne saw that it was the old man who was occupying the room from which he had seen the car outside the Hall. He grinned with relief and the barrel of the shotgun started to drop. Then he realised that the old man held something in his other hand. It was a revolver. Arne stood motionless, his mind working speedily over the possible explanations. He tried to remember what his impression of the old man had been. None came readily to mind. The only thing that was clear was that he had spoken with a London accent. Earlier that evening he had received a telephone call and had immediately made a call himself. The name he had registered under was Sidney Carver. There was nothing about the man that explained the gun. Suddenly the torch beam moved and caught Arne.

'It's me Arne,' he said quickly, but the gun in the man's hand came up and Arne hesitated no longer. He flung himself sideways as the old man pressed the trigger of the revolver. The

149

roar was magnified as it echoed in the confined space of the small room. Then Arne hit the floor and didn't waste any more time on niceties. He squeezed one of the triggers and the blast caught the old man in the chest and flung him backwards out of the room and into the hallway. Arne came to his feet and reached for the telephone. The tinny voice was silent.

'Are you still there?' Arne asked.

'Yes. Was that a shot?'

'Never mind that. Listen...' There was a click and the telephone went dead. Arne stood for a second or two listening, but there was nothing. Just silence. Abruptly he dropped the instrument onto the desk and crossed to the door. He flicked the light switch on and immediately off again. It was enough to show him where the old man's torch had fallen and he picked it up and used it to locate the revolver. He stepped over the body and went down the hallway to the door that led into the car park. His car was standing where he had left it when Blake had moved his Landrover and Arne climbed in and drove out slowly into Stonor Lane. He reasoned that if the two men he had seen had taken the Fawley road, then with gunfire coming from the direction of Lower Assendon, the only possible way out of the village by road had to be that one. He passed the row of four cottages and saw two villagers standing at a doorway looking towards the village centre. He went straight on past them and towards the hump-backed bridge that spanned the small stream. He was within a few yards of the bridge when he saw two figures, one in the centre of the road, waving to him to stop and the other by the wall of the bridge. In his headlights he saw they both wore army-style combat suits and both were armed. He flicked the lights onto full beam and saw their faces. He reached sideways and picked up the shotgun from the passenger seat and then without pause he opened the car door and threw himself out onto the roadway. He rolled over and scrambled for the cover of the trees by the side of the road. He heard shouts behind him and then shots were fired and he heard the grating of metal against stone as the car scraped into the bridge and stopped. The car's engine was still running and he took advantage of the noise to make a run for it, heedless of the noise he was making as he crashed through the small copse. Then there was silence as the engine was switched off. He stopped and listened. He could hear no sound of anyone moving in the woods behind him and he began to move forward again, this time slowly and cautiously. It took him ten minutes to reach the far end of the wood and he peered out towards the Fawley Road. On the bridge that spanned the same stream were two figures and he assumed they were the men who had killed Blake. Arne crouched on his heels and then after a moment he moved off to his right and began to make his way back towards the village centre. When he was almost back at the car park of the Oak he carefully crossed the Fawley road and began to move to the east, up the hill that led towards the Hall. He had decided that with the village seemingly cut-off it was about time he discovered just what was happening at Fenton Hall.

CHAPTER SEVENTEEN

The small convoy of police cars had just passed the sixth exit from the motorway when a call came in from the Yard headquarters. The caller was Police Constable Mather, linked through from the office from where he was co-ordinating messages until the cars reached the Fenton Oak, where it was Mason's intention to set up an incident centre. The driver of the leading car passed the microphone back to the Chief Superintendent.

'Go ahead Mather,' Mason said.

'I've just taken a call from the owner of the Fenton Oak sir.'

'What did he want?'

'I don't know sir. He came on the line, mentioned Police Constable Blake's name, then he seemed to put down the telephone. I tried to talk to him but he didn't answer. Then there was a shot . . .'

'A shot? You're sure?'

'Well I think . . . no sir, I'm sure it was a shot. Then Mr. Arne came back on the line but before he had time to tell me what had happened the 'phone went dead.'

'Have you tried to regain contact?'

'We're trying now sir but . . . just a moment sir.' There was a pause and Mason stared straight ahead through the windscreen. Beside him Ted Armstrong impatiently tapped his fingers on his knee. When Mather's voice came back over the speaker both men jumped involuntarily. 'The G.P.O. have just told us that both the Hambledon and Fenton exchanges have failed. They don't know why.'

'Okay Mather, call me if you re-make contact.'

'Yes sir.' Mason reached forward and handed the microphone to the driver who pushed it into its clip under his dashboard. Mason leaned back and rubbed at his face first with one hand and then with the other.

'Could be a coincidence I suppose,' Armstrong said.

'Do you think it is?' Mason asked.

'No.'

'Neither do I. But I have to admit I can't see Dave Lorrimar for this.'

'He's a big boy now Arthur. Maybe he really

153

is pulling the one big tickle they all dream about.'

'Maybe. But think about it Ted. He has made no attempt to hide the fact that he was interested in the place. If he is there, at the Hall, holding the Garroways prisoner, as we are both inclined to think is the case, then taking out an entire telephone exchange doesn't fit. Garroway has told Klein he will be in the office on Monday and Klein has confirmed that to release cash of this magnitude Garroway's presence is necessary. That means the gang, if there is one, plan to let Sir James leave the Hall on Monday. They must have accepted that he cannot keep what is happening a secret. They expect us to find out about them, maybe not as fast as we have, but they expect it all the same.'

'So?'

'So why cut the telephone? In fact, I would think a telephone link to the outside world would be vital for them. But let's assume for a moment they did want the telephone to the Hall cutting off, all they have to do is snip through the wires at the inside of the Hall. They don't have to cut off the entire exchange.'

'You've almost convinced me the exchange going out of action is a coincidence.'

'Except that you're like me Ted. You don't believe in coincidences.'

'They do happen.'

'But not very often.'

154

'Maybe.' Armstrong thought for a moment. 'You know what? You're trying to have it both ways. You want to believe that Lorrimar is holed up there holding the Garroways to ransom, but you don't want to believe he's cut off the telephones in the area.'

'Yes. Doesn't make a lot of sense does it?'

'No.'

'Okay, let's play at being policemen and stop speculating. We'll wait until we get to Fenton and find out for ourselves.'

There were three cars in the convoy. Mason and Armstrong were in the leading car with a driver, the other cars each carried four men, all of whom were armed. Mason resumed staring ahead, over the driver's shoulder, watching the motorway unwind in the headlights. They had reached the M4 spur and were turning off to join the A423 when Mather called again. The driver passed the microphone to Mason once more.

'Go ahead Mather.'

'Mr. Maxwell wants a word with you sir. Says it's very important.'

'Put him on.' Mason listened to the clicks as the connection was made.

'Hello,' Maxwell's papery voice crackled in the confined space of the car.

'Hello Max. What have you got?'

'Another link with Fenton. A good day for coincidences.' Mason looked at Armstrong and raised an eyebrow.

155

'Go on, he said into the microphone.

'There's a big do on in Reading tonight.'

'Yes, I had heard. The local Chief Constable is there.'

'Maybe, he certainly isn't the biggest of the big noises who'll be there.'

'Who is?'

'Royalty.' Mason's fingers clenched vice-like around the microphone.

'Who?' he asked.

'Next but one in line of succession no less.' Mason held his breath for a moment.

'Where does Fenton come in?'

'He is escorting a young lady for the evening. Sarah Garroway. He was due to pick her up at Fenton Hall at about eight this evening.' There was a long silence before Mason spoke again.

'Thanks Max,' he said. 'Re-connect me with Mather will you?'

'Righto.' The clicks rattled in the loudspeaker and then Mather came back on the line.

'Yes sir?'

'Did you hear any of that Mather?'

'Yes sir,' Mason noted the tension in the young constable's voice.

'Make contact with the Commissioner. Emergency procedure. And Mather.'

'Yes sir.'

'You're about to be replaced. Sorry lad, don't let it worry you, no reflection on your ability.'

'No sir.' Mason held the microphone loosely

in his lap until he heard Mather's voice again.

'Go ahead,' he told the constable.

'I have the Commissioner on the line sir.'

'Put him on.' Mason listened to the clicking again and this time the sound seemed to carry a warning of impending danger that had not been there before. When the Commissioner came on the line Mason began to speak in terse, emotionless sentences. He talked until the car was well past Henley and was approaching the village of Lower Assendon.

CHAPTER EIGHTEEN

The Hall was quiet. The Garroway family and their visitors were in the main bedroom. Hart was on the landing, armed with his own .44 Smith & Wesson and with Mannion's .32. McKendrick was in the garden at the back of the house, positioned so that he could see the windows of the bedrooms. He carried his own Beretta and a Walther PPK semi-automatic, one of the spare weapons the gang had brought with them. Lorrimar and Mannion were in the kitchen and, with the exception of the weapons still hidden in the greenhouse behind the garage, the gang's fire power was cluttered between them on the kitchen table. Two AKM rifles, the ugly Ceska 7.5 millimetre automatic

157

and a six-shot .32 Smith & Wesson Lorrimar had taken from the smaller of the two men Sarah Garroway had tried to warn against coming to the house. Lorrimar's own weapon lay between his hands, the barrel pointing significantly at Mannion who sat facing the taller man, his face gleaming with sweat in the bright fluorescent light. His small eyes kept flickering from gun to gun, never once lifting to look at Lorrimar.

'Okay Ken.' Lorrimar's voice was soft and menacing. 'Let's try again. You knew the Prince would be here tonight didn't you?' Mannion twisted in his seat. 'Didn't you?' Lorrimar's voice cracked out.

'Y . . . Yes,' Mannion stammered.

'Explain.' Lorrimar's voice was quiet again.

'I heard at the last minute, I thought . . . I didn't want us to lose the chance.'

'I don't believe you Ken.'

'I didn't know he would be calling here for her. I thought she would be meeting him elsewhere. I thought we could get her to make a telephone call and . . .' Mannion's voice trailed off. He stared in silence at the assorted weapons on the table.

'Still lying Ken. You knew he would be here and you thought it would make for better bargaining power. You bloody fool. What do you think will happen now, when he doesn't show up at the dinner in Reading? And what about the other guy, the bodyguard?'

158

Lorrimar's finger jabbed at the gun he had taken from the second man. 'Martin, the copper, what do you think will happen when he doesn't report in? It won't be just the coppers, it'll be the army, the air force and, if they can get them up here, the bloody navy as well.' He stared at Mannion, his face impassive but his eyes wide with anger. 'Well?'

'I didn't know he'd come here Dave. Look we can still do it. We can still go ahead.'

'Of course we can't. I wasn't joking when I said they'd send in the military.'

'We can't back out now. They know us, the Garroways know our names. We have to go on.' Lorrimar looked at Mannion and suddenly he leaned forward.

'You made a telephone call tonight. Who to?'

'I didn't . . .'

'Bill heard you make it. Who did you call?'

'I called Sid.'

'Why?'

'Just to tell him that all was going well.'

'Why? What does he need to know for?'

'I . . . I just wanted to tell him . . . so that he could go ahead with the sale of the cottage.' Lorrimar leaned back in his chair. Then he stood up and without taking his eyes off the fat man he walked to the window and waved into the darkness. McKendrick came into the kitchen a few moments later.

'Watch him Bill,' Lorrimar said. He gathered

159

up all the weapons and let the little man open the door into the passage. He went up the stairs and dumped the guns on the half-landing. Then he went on up to the landing where Hart was leaning against the wall facing the door to the main bedroom.

'Has he told you anything?' Hart asked.

'No. Still sticking to the tale that he didn't expect him to come here.'

'Do you believe him?'

'I don't know Jim. He isn't a fool. He must have known we would be in trouble if he showed up here.'

'Where does it leave us?'

'I don't know that either. If we hang around here much longer someone is bound to start wondering where he is,' Lorrimar jerked his thumb at the bedroom door. 'And if we go, every copper in the country will be after us before we've gone half a mile down the road. We'll have no helicopter, no aircraft, no money, nothing.'

'I've been thinking,' Hart said.

'What?'

'We could get Garroway out here. Tell him the truth, that we didn't know about the Prince. He'll believe that, he must have reckoned we didn't know about it from the start.'

'Then what?'

'Tell him we want out. Lay on the helicopter and the Cessna and some working cash. Not four million, just enough to get us moving. He might play along.' Lorrimar thought for a moment.

'Won't work Jim. He probably would go along, but what would happen when the police find out? They won't let us get away with it. A member of the Royal Family. Even if we get out now we're still liable for holding him against his will, threatening him with a weapon. Christ, they'll find ways of keeping us inside until we're too old to walk.'

'With the Cessna we can follow our original plan. Go where we intended going.'

'No, Jim. Holding a financier to ransom is one thing. Where we were going they wouldn't have allowed extradition proceedings against us for that. But this, no, we're in the mire, well and truly.' The two men stood silently for a moment then Hart turned his head slightly.

'Listen,' he said. He stepped up to the door of one of the bedrooms at the front of the house, opened it, went in and crossed to the window. He opened the curtains and looked out. Then he opened the window. Lorrimar remained at the door, half-turned to keep the main bedroom's door under observation.

'What is it?' he asked.

'Aircraft of some kind. Wait.' Hart leaned out of the window and Lorrimar heard the sound clearly. Hart stepped back and closed the window. He turned and looked at Lorrimar.

161

'Helicopter,' he said. 'Maybe two of them. Coming down somewhere near, could be in the field by the churchyard.' Lorrimar looked at the taller man.

'The army,' he said. 'The police must have found out and called in the army. Jesus.'

'We'd better get out Dave, and fast.' Lorimar nodded.

'Come on,' he said. 'Keep it quiet, don't let them hear us in there. We don't want them to know we're pulling out.' He went down the stairs, moving silently and Hart followed him. On the half-landing Lorrimar picked up one of the rifles and one of the hand guns. Behind him he heard Hart pick up the other AKM and the remaining automatic. Lorrimar went into the kitchen. 'Right, Bill, we're getting out.' The little man looked up.

'Okay,' he said. 'What about him?' he pointed to Mannion.

'You'd better come with us Ken. God knows I'd like to leave you, but there's nothing to be gained by it. The army won't ease up on us because they've got you.'

'Army?' McKendrick said.

'Yes, there's one, maybe two helicopters just landed in the field across the road. Must be the army.' Lorrimar stopped, looking hard at Mannion, the fat man's expression became non-committal, but not before Lorrimar had identified the look that had passed over his face.

162

Mannion had looked relieved. Lorrimar tried to answer the questions that leaped into his mind. Then he shook his head, he was wasting time. 'Bill,' he said. 'Get the rest of the gear.' McKendrick nodded and slipped out of the door and into the garden. Lorrimar turned to Hart. 'Switch off the light Jim,' he said. He crossed to the door and looked out into the darkness. 'Okay Ken,' he said. 'You first, straight across to the woods at the bottom of the garden. Try anything, anything at all and I'll kill you.' His voice was low and expressionless and there was no doubt that he meant what he said. The fat man started across the lawn with Lorrimar behind him. Hart followed and a few moments later McKendrick drifted towards them from the direction of the greenhouse. All four men heard the burst of firing quite clearly.

'Hold it,' Lorrimar said. He turned to Hart. 'That came from some way off. Further than the field by the church.'

'Yes, it was down towards the main road.'

'What was it? Sounded like a machine gun of some kind.'

'Could be. High-pitched sound. Could have been one of several things.'

'What the hell are the army doing firing over there? Christ look at that.' He pointed and McKendrick and Hart saw the glow rising into the sky and then there was a low rumbling explosion. Lorrimar turned suddenly and saw

163

that Mannion was still moving across the lawn. 'Bill,' he snapped. 'Get him back here.' McKendrick dropped the case he was carrying and scuttled after the fat man. 'Jim, this isn't making sense.' Lorrimar said to Hart. 'What's going on?'

'Could be diversions. Trying to make us think they're not after us.'

'Why would they do that for God's sake?'

'Don't know,' Hart admitted. Then they heard more shots, this time from the direction of the village. Lorrimar looked at Hart and then at Mannion as he came up, prodded by McKendrick.

'Right,' he said. 'Back into the house.' He set off towards the darkened shape, the only light coming from the upstairs window of the main bedroom. Behind him he heard the others follow. At the house he went in through the kitchen door and without pausing he went straight through and into the hall. He ran up the stairs and opened the door to the bedroom. The six people in the room looked at him. He reached in and rested his hand on the light switch.

'Keep away from the windows,' he said and turned off the light. He closed the door and went back down the stairs. As he reached the hallway Hart opened the kitchen door. 'Dining-room Jim,' he said. 'See what you can see.'

'Right,' Hart said. Lorrimar walked into the

kitchen. In the darkness he could make out the shadowy shape of McKendrick standing by the back door. Mannion was at the table and Lorrimar having walked straight up to the fat man smashed his fist into his face. There was a wet thud and then Mannion was on the floor moaning, the sound muffled by his hands which were clasped to his face. Lorrimar knelt by his side.

'Who's out there?' he asked. The fat man moaned softly. Lorrimar dragged him into a sitting position and hit him again, this time an open-handed slap across the face. 'Who is it?' he asked. 'I won't ask again Ken. I'll destroy you.' Mannion squirmed and then as Lorrimar raised his hand again he nodded his head rapidly.

'Okay, okay. Look Dave, I'm not double-crossing you, you're in it. All of you. Jim and Bill. It's all as before except that we get the four million from Garroway and we get another four million from them.'

'From who?'

'The men in the helicopters.'

'Why will they give us another four million?' There was silence in the kitchen broken only by Mannion's breathing. 'Why?' asked Lorrimar softly.

'For him,' Mannion said. Lorrimar stared at him in disbelief.

'You stupid bastard,' he said. 'Who are they for Christ's sake?'

'They're an organisation, I don't know their names, I've only met one of them. He made the offer and helped with the set-up.' Lorrimar looked up at McKendrick.

'Sorry mate,' he said. 'Looks as if we're in a spot.'

'Not your fault Dave,' the little man said. 'What do we do now?'

'It's two million quid Bill,' Mannion said. 'Think of it, two million. You could live on that for ever.'

'I could have lived for ever on one,' McKendrick said. 'And I wouldn't have got shot at. Haven't you heard of treason you stupid sod?'

'Oh, he's heard of it alright,' Lorrimar said. 'But he reckoned that he could stand that kind of pressure with all that money. And I don't mean two millions either. You just threw that in for weight didn't you Ken? You never intended us having a cut. Your mates out there were going to give us the chop. Right? Then you'd clear off, forget the Garroway money, that was all part of the set-up. There never was any intention of letting that deal go ahead. Your friends out there would take the Prince and you and go. Right? Only if you thought they'd let you live to spend it you must be even more stupid than I think.' He stood up. 'Get up,' he said, digging the fat man in the ribs with his toe. 'You still haven't told me who they are.'

166

'I told you I don't know.'

'And I don't believe you. Now tell me or I'll finish you now.'

'The man I dealt with is called Okada Kurusu.' Lorrimar looked at him for a moment.

'Are they all Japanese?'

'Yes.'

'Terrorists?'

'Yes.'

'Jesus. How many are out there?'

'I don't know Dave, straight I don't.'

'You said helicopters. How many?'

'Two, they needed to know that the field was big enough to set two down.'

'Right, could be six to twelve men. Bill, tie his hands. Use his tie. Be quick.' The little man did as Lorrimar instructed and then Lorrimar pushed Mannion into a chair. 'Any trouble Bill and . . .'

'I know,' McKendrick said. Lorrimar went up the stairs hurriedly. He opened the door of the bedroom, flicked on the light switch to check that none of the men were close to the door and then switched off the light again.

'Listen carefully,' he said. Hastily he outlined what had taken place in the past few minutes. No one spoke until he had finished.

'Do you know who the men are?' the tall young man asked calmly.

'No,' Lorrimar said. 'Only that they are Japanese terrorists. If they're anything like the

167

crowd that attacked Tel Aviv airport a few years back then we've got problems.'

'And there is no doubt that they want me?'

'Seems not.' The young man came closer to Lorrimar.

'Then perhaps we had better talk to them. There is no sense in everyone here being harmed.'

'No,' Lorrimar said. 'Look, I'm not trying to set myself up as anything I'm not. I came here to hold the Garroways to ransom for money. I've done banks and post offices and all the rest and I've broken a few bones in my time and maybe worse, but I'm not going for this. This is something else. Anyway, if you hand yourself over what makes you think they'll quietly go away? If they are anything like that other mob they'll wipe us out for the fun of it.'

'I still . . .'

'No,' Lorrimar interrupted. 'No arguments. Now listen. All of you are coming downstairs. The women will all go into the cloakroom. There are no windows in there. The others will help with the defence. We've enough fire power to keep them away for a while. So long as they are trying to take you alive, that is. With luck the police or the army will be here before they lose patience.' He turned to Martin, the bodyguard.

'Do you agree?' The man did not hesitate.

'Yes,' he said. 'But no deals for afterwards.'

168

Lorrimar's teeth gleamed in the darkness.

'Once a copper always a bloody copper,' he said and turned and led the way down the stairs. On the ground floor he hurried Lady Garroway and her two daughters into the cloakroom. Then he led the others to the dining-room. Hart was crouched by the window, the curtains drawn together but hooked up so that he could see beneath them out into the grounds. 'Anything Jim?' Lorrimar asked.

'No.' Hart turned round and looked at the others. He looked enquiringly at Lorrimar.

'Mannion set us up mate,' he said. 'There's a crowd of terrorists out there, Japanese. They're after him', he jerked a thumb at the Prince. 'We've changed sides for the time being. Okay?' Hart grinned easily.

'Have I any choice?'

'Not a lot. The chances are they're all set to eliminate us anyway, so we might as well do our best to stall them until the police get here.'

'Christ, I never thought the day would come when I would want to see the law.' Hart grinned, 'Okay Dave you're the boss,' he went on.

'Not on this kind of deal Jim. You'd better take charge.' Lorrimar turned to Martin.

'Try the telephone, if there's a line, call your lads. Chances are it'll be cut. That's what I would have done if I was out there.' The policeman crossed the room, picked up one of the telephones and listened.

'Dead,' he said.

'Okay,' Lorrimar said. 'Listen all of you. For the rest of this little lot we take orders from Jim here. All of us and that includes me and it includes you,' he pointed at the Prince. The young man looked at him and nodded unsmilingly. Hart uncoiled himself from the floor.

'Right,' he said. 'We'd do better from upstairs, but we can't risk them getting into the house. Where are the women Dave?'

'In the cloakroom.'

'Good. And the rest of the shooters?'

'In the kitchen.'

'Get them will you Dave?' Lorrimar went out of the room. 'Okay, let's move fast. I want one man in the sitting-room at the window. That's you Sir James. We'll fix you up with an AKM. It's a Russian rifle. There'll be a hand gun as well in case you come under extreme pressure. Draw the curtains and turn up the bottoms like these here. Then if they fire into the windows the broken glass won't hit anyone and there's a chance that the bullets might get stopped as well. Depends on what they're using. Anyway some of the velocity will be lost. Might make a difference between an ordinary wound and a fatal one.' He stopped as Lorrimar came in. Hart handed one of the rifles to Sir James and added the five shot .32 he had taken from

Mannion. 'Okay, get moving. Keep the door open so we can all talk to one another if we need to. I'll bring extra ammunition to you later. You,' he motioned to the policeman, 'Take your own Smith & Wesson and the other AKM. You take this window, right?'

'Right,' Martin said.

'We'll leave Bill where he is Dave. What's he got?'

'His Beretta and the Walther.'

'Okay, they're both nine millimetre, that'll keep life simple there. You take the breakfast-room windows Dave. Can you manage both of them?' Lorrimar glanced down the length of the dining-room and through into the breakfast-room.

'Yes, unless they make a major assault there.'

'Okay, you've got your .44?'

'Yes.'

'Right, take mine as well. Simplifies the ammo again.' Lorrimar moved away down the room.

'That leaves you and me chief,' Hart remarked cheerfully to the Prince. 'Seeing you're the target you'd better keep your head well down...'

'Wait a moment...'

'No, you listen. As long as you're alive the rest of us have a chance. Not good, but a chance. As soon as they decide you're dead, or probably dead, the rest of us will be

171

supernumerary. They'll blow us away without a second's thought. We don't know what they've got out there, but even light artillery isn't an impossibility.'

'But...'

'No, I don't want you down here. Go upstairs, open all the doors to all the bedrooms. Keep moving from room to room. Keep low and don't leave your head in view for more than a few seconds. If you see anything at all then sing out. Loud as well. We all need to hear. Okay?' There was only the slightest pause before the young man nodded.

'Yes,' he said and turned away.

'Wait,' Hart said. 'You'll need this.' He handed the Prince the Ceska automatic. 'Bit elderly I'm afraid, but it works and it will frighten them even if it misses.' He grinned in the darkness and after a moment the young man smiled and nodded his head. He went quietly out of the room. Hart turned to Martin. 'Will he be okay?' he asked. Martin looked round.

'Yes,' he said simply. Hart nodded and picked up the suitcase and went down to where Lorrimar was looking through the windows of the breakfast-room. Hart laid the case on the floor and snapped open the catches. He lifted out the contents and laid them side by side next to the case. He glanced up at Lorrimar.

'I suppose we're doing the right thing,' he said.

'We're doing the only thing we can do,' Lorrimar answered.

'I expect you're right.' He picked up one of the weapons. 'Used one of these before Dave?' Lorrimar glanced down.

'No. Armalite isn't it?'

'Yes. Watch me.' Hart showed the other man the principle of the weapon and then handed it to him. 'Okay?'

'Yes. The others are the same?'

'Yes. One for me and one for Bill or whoever needs it most.'

'Right. What's in the box, ammunition?'

'Some. There's also a few equalisers.' Hart lifted the lid of the box Lorrimar had pointed at. Lorrimar looked inside.

'Hand grenades. Christ, did you expect this was going to happen?'

'No, but aren't you glad I have a nasty turn of mind?' Lorrimar grinned.

'Yes,' he said. 'Look, have a word with Bill, put him in the picture and we'd better have Mannion where we can see him. Bring him in here. Put him in one of the chairs at the table.'

'Right.' Hart picked up one of the Armalite rifles and went out into the kitchen. He showed McKendrick how to use the semi-automatic weapon and then prodded Mannion to his feet and took him into the dining-room. He made the fat man sit at the table and then pulled his already bound hands to a position where he could tie them to the back of the chair. Then he went back to Lorrimar.

'Okay Dave. I'm going outside. I need to have a quick look round. Best we know what's happening out there.' Lorrimar nodded his head.

'Okay Jim. This is turning out to be your operation. Do what you think is best.'

'I'll find something darker to wear then I'll go out of the kitchen door and make my way around the house this way then round to the front and back again in through the kitchen door. I'll tell the others what I'm up to so they don't start firing at me. Come to that I think we ought to have a rule. Let them shoot first. Two reasons. One is they don't know how well fixed we are for guns. The other is that there just might be somebody else out there apart from Mannion's little yellow friends.'

'Okay. Take care mate.' Lorrimar watched Hart move silently down the room to speak to Martin, then he disappeared through the dining-room door. Lorrimar turned to peer out into the darkness. He could see no movements and he could hear nothing. The thought drifted into his mind that the whole thing might turn out to be a complete mistake and that there might be a perfectly rational explanation for the firing they had heard earlier. Then he dismissed the thought. Whatever was happening outside it wasn't likely to be rational. Far from it, it was

174

probably completely irrational and worse, very likely fatal to more than one of them.

CHAPTER NINETEEN

The two soldiers had reached the cover of the woods and Webb told Manning to stay out of sight. The lieutenant moved off silently but quickly, moving parallel to the road they had been on when the ambush had occurred and still heading towards the village they had originally been approaching. He saw the helicopters when he was about three hundred yards away from them. He dropped into a crouch and considered the terrain. The helicopters were in a field and he could make out the tower of a church a short distance beyond. Where he was, on the edge of the wood, he was above the level of the field. That gave him one small advantage. The other was surprise. There was a reasonable chance that the enemy had assumed that all the occupants of the Landrover had been inside when it had blown up. In any event there was reason to assume that if anyone stood guard over the helicopters they didn't know about the attack on the Landrover. They would have heard the firing and the explosion, but there was some doubt that they would be aware of what had actually happened. Webb began to move down the hill, more cautiously as he left the protecting cover of the trees. He had reached the wire fence that surrounded the field before he saw anyone. There was one man, kneeling between the two machines. As Webb froze into immobility the man made a slow turn through three hundred and sixty degrees and then resumed his position, looking away from where Webb crouched. Webb slipped under the bottom wire of the fence and began a slow crawl towards the man. Only once did the man look around again and Webb, seeing the movement begin, buried his face in his arms. After a moment he risked an upwards glance and saw that the man had settled into his position again, his back to Webb. This time Webb did not move at once. Instead he considered his options. He had no idea if the man was alone. As far as he could see there was no one else on the ground, but that left the helicopters. Any number of men could still be in there. Abruptly he made up his mind. He came up into a crouch and moved quickly towards the man, the SLR ready. He was within ten feet of the man before he moved. As the figure turned and began to rise Webb leaped forward two long strides and struck upwards with the rifle. The muzzle caught the man in the throat and as he went backwards gagging and choking, Webb, still moving with the impetus of his leap, sank one boot into the man's stomach and then swung the butt of the rifle against the side of his head. He dropped to his knees by the side of the man and listened. He heard nothing. He pulled the man over onto his back and looked at his face. The man was oriental, but Webb was unsure whether he was Chinese or Japanese, or even something else entirely. There was a weapon on the wet grass and Webb picked it up and tried to think of a simple way around the next problem. The man on the ground solved it for him. He groaned suddenly and Webb swung the SLR down and again smashed it against the man's temple. There was a sickening, cracking sound and the man was still. Webb knelt over him and put his face close to the man's lips. There seemed to be no breath. He felt slightly sick and then he remembered the screams from the two men who had died in the front of the Landrover. He moved quickly and silently to the first machine and looked in through the open doorway. Then he ducked down and ran round to the second helicopter. Moments later he was rapidly back-tracking towards where he had left Manning. The rifleman saw him when he was still some distance away and moved towards him. Webb saw the movement and stopped and waited.

'Everything okay sir?' Manning asked as he came up to the lieutenant.

'Yes. Only one guard on the helicopters. This was his. You'd better have my SLR. I'll use

177

this, I think it's a Russian AK 47. If it's what they used on McIntosh and Lowe it will be effective.' Webb glanced down the hill. 'Okay,' he went on. 'We don't know who they are or what they're doing here. The fellow I took this off was Chinese or maybe Japanese, I'm not certain. So we can't begin to guess what they're up to. Now, the helicopters are over there towards the village. The ambush was down there about half a mile south of the village. As far as we know there's no one this side of the road so whatever they're after is either in the village or over there on the hill at the other side of the road. Seems likely the village is the target. The ambush wasn't just a road block. They're trying to cut-off the village so I think we should concentrate on that. We'll go down and have a look.' Manning looked at the lieutenant.

'But there's only two of us sir.'

'Yes, but they think we're dead.'

'Shouldn't we try to get help?'

'Yes, and we will, but not yet. Our radio's out of action and there's a good chance they'll have put the telephones out. That means that to get to a 'phone that's working we might have to go a long way.'

'The main road's only a half mile sir. We can commandeer a car.'

'Yes, and we will, or rather you will, just as soon as we've dealt with another little matter.'

'What's that?'

178

'We're going to put their transport out of action. With these helicopters out of commision it keeps them here while help is coming. Right? Follow me.' The young officer began to move down the way he had returned from the field by the church and the rifleman followed.

★   ★   ★

Simon Arne had reached a position where he could see the Hall. The building was in darkness. He lay motionless in the long grass, his head up, with his hands cupped around his eyes to cut out sideways vision. After several minutes he moved forward again, wriggling along, his shotgun cradled across his arms, the pistol he had taken from the old man he had killed at the Oak dragging uncomfortably in the pocket of his anorak. After he had moved forward about five yards he stopped and again looked all around, listening carefully before he cautiously moved forward another five yards. He continued slowly up the slope stopping every so often but he neither saw nor heard anything. He continued until he reached a position where he was almost due north of the Hall, still in long grass, but on more level ground. He carefully eased himself into a position where he could assess the layout. He had never been in that part of the grounds of the Hall, but he was reasonably certain that apart from a small

179

shrubbery there was nothing between him and the building. He knew that the long grass would turn into closer cut lawn a little further on. He had decided to risk a further forward movement which would bring him nearer the side of the garage when he saw something move round from the back of the house. It was a man. As he watched, the figure moved out towards him in a wide sweep and was momentarily hidden from sight behind a raised flower bed. Arne stayed where he was, motionless. Then the figure re-appeared and came closer. Soon the man was within a few yards of his position. He could see that the man was tall, although moving in a crouch and he could also see that he was carrying something in his hands. Arne shifted his position slightly and gently eased the automatic from his pocket. He had prepared to take the man as he passed in front of him when suddenly from his right there was a short burst of automatic rifle fire. Arne flung himself flat once again. Ahead of him he heard a scream. The tall man had been hit. Arne heard the soft swishing sound of someone moving on wet grass. He saw a figure approach where the man lay on the ground. Then there were two shots blending into one as the man on the ground and the second man fired simultaneously. The second man was catapulted backwards and disappeared from Arne's sight. There was silence. After a few long moments Arne heard a soft whistle from well to the right, the direction the second man had come from. Then there was silence again. Cautiously Arne moved forward towards where the tall man had fallen. When he reached him the man was lying on his side, breathing in jerky gasps. There was an automatic rifle in his hands and Arne eased himself to a position where the man could not hit him if he pressed the trigger involuntarily. He leaned over the man's head.

'Can you hear me?' he whispered. The head moved slightly. 'Where are you hit?' The head moved again and there was a faint rattling sound in the man's throat as he tried to speak.

'Everywhere,' he whispered.

'What's happening?' Arne asked.

'The Hall. Defending against them outside.'

'Who's attacking?'

'Terrorists.'

'Why?' There was no reply. Arne pressed his fingers into the man's neck and felt for a pulse. There was none. Carefully Arne took the rifle from the dead man's grasp and, leaving his shotgun by the body, he crawled to where the other man lay. Cautiously he poked at the man with the muzzle of the rifle. There was no response and he crawled closer and looked into the man's face. Even in the darkness Arne knew the man was dead. A bullet had hit him in the face. There wasn't a lot of the face left but what there was looked Japanese. Arne glanced towards where he had heard the whistle. He could see nothing. He took the second man's weapon and began to move on again towards the house.

CHAPTER TWENTY

As the three police cars turned into the lane that led to Fenton village, Detective Chief Superintendent Arthur Mason leaned forward and spoke to the driver.

'Stop here,' he said. The car slowed and Mason twisted round in his seat to look through the rear window. When the following cars had stopped he opened the door and clambered out. With Chief Superintendent Armstrong he hurried back and gestured to the rest of the squad to gather for a hasty conference.

'We have a problem,' he said, his voice pitched low. 'There is reason to believe that a member of the Royal Family is at the Hall and that his life is in danger.' He paused to let his words sink in. 'A major incident centre is being set up and our original plans to run the show from the local pub have been abandoned. The local Task Force is being mobilised and a unit is on its way now. All available local men are being gathered up for a mass sweep on the area. There are four more units on their way from the Met.

Two of ours, one from the Bomb Squad, just in case, and one from the Special Commando. The Army are being brought in, but for the moment we don't know who is nearest and we don't know how long they'll take getting here. Our duties are to reconnoitre the area and prepare basic data for an assault on the Hall, if that becomes necessary.' He paused again and rubbed his hands together. 'We're splitting up, in case we run into problems. I want one car to make a quick pass through the village. Jackson, that's you. Whatever you see, don't stop, just keep on going and report back later. The second car, you take that one Ted, will take the first turning on the right down here. That will take you down to Remenham village. From there you can get to Fawley and then you can come back into Fenton from the north-east. Report back to me by radio but use non-committal language. Nothing that will give away what we're doing. That's in case they're listening to our frequency. Any questions?' No one spoke, the men shuffled their feet trying to keep warm. 'Okay Jackson, get started.' Inspector Jackson climbed back into the second car, three others got in with him and the driver started the engine and pulled around the leading car. Mason drew Armstrong to one side. 'While you're going round the block I'll take a quick run down to Lower Assendon, try the telephone there. It may be just the pub's 'phone that's off, but it could be they've put the area out.'

'Okay Arthur. That should be . . .'

'Car coming sir,' one of the men called out. The two senior officers turned as a car came down towards them from the direction of Fenton.

'It's Jackson,' Armstrong said. The car stopped and Jackson wound down his window and leaned out.

'Just before the turn off to Remenham there's a burned out Landrover, still smouldering so it's happened recently. Beyond it, past the junction there's a barricade across the road with a detour sign to Remenham. Looks official, but I expect it isn't.'

'Anyone about?'

'Didn't see anyone, but we didn't stop to look.' Mason nodded his head and thought for a moment.

'Let's have a look at the map again,' he said to the driver. The map was spread over the bonnet of Jackson's car. 'Okay,' Mason said after a moment. 'We can send the second car the way we intended. That's you Ted, take it slowly as you pass the Landrover, see if you can make out anything and keep your eyes well-peeled for anyone hanging about. Jackson, you go back down onto the main road, turn right and go into Bix. There's a lane there,' his finger jabbed at the map. 'It will bring you out onto the road between Fenton and Stonor. Approach the village from there. Drop one of your men off in Lower Assendon, get him to check the telephones there and then walk back up here to me.' He turned to Armstrong. 'Ted, there'll be five of you in that car. When you get about half a mile up the lane from the corner there drop two men off. If they can block the road with anything tell them to do so. If they can't then they stop the first car that comes along and use that to block the road. When you reach a position on the Fawley road approaching the village block the road. Jackson, you do the same on the Stonor road. If whoever is in there is stopping us from getting in, then the least we can do is stop them from getting out. Okay, everyone, get moving.' The men crowded back into their cars and the two vehicles moved off, one towards the main road, the other towards Fenton. Mason watched the car that was approaching the village, he waited until he saw from the configuration of its lights that it had turned to the right into Remenham Lane. Then he turned to his driver. 'Right, block the road. I don't know what caused that Landrover to burn out but we'll play it safe. We'll stay outside the car.' He waited until the driver had repositioned the car and then he scrambled into the hedge at the roadside. 'Take the other side of the road,' he said. 'From now, don't talk unless you have to.'

CHAPTER TWENTY-ONE

Lorrimar had not seen Hart move past the breakfast-room windows, but he knew that he was somewhere in the grounds as the tall man had been gone for almost twenty minutes. Then he heard the burst of firing and the scream and he risked putting his face close to the north-facing window and tried vainly to see what was happening outside. Then he heard another sound and this time he was unsure whether it was one shot or two. He waited and heard nothing more. Martin looked down the room towards Lorrimar.

'See anything?' he asked.

'No. You?'

'No.'

'Below,' the voice came from upstairs.

'Yes,' Lorrimar called out.

'Someone approaching from the north. One man.'

'Right,' Lorrimar called. 'I'll take care of him. Check the other sides. Fast.' He resumed his position and it was several minutes before he saw someone crawling over the grass towards the house. He tried to see if it was Hart, but it was just a black, featureless shape. He remembered Hart's order to let the men outside the house shoot first. He waited. It could be

Hart, wounded perhaps.

'See anyone?' Martin called softly.

'Yes. Can't make out if it's Jim or not.'

'Don't take any chances Lorrimar,' the policeman said.

'I'm not shooting until I'm sure it isn't Jim.'

'That isn't . . .'

'Quiet,' Lorrimar hissed. 'I think he's calling.' He reached behind him for one of the .44 Smith & Wessons and swung the weapon up and smashed one of the panes of glass in the window. He dropped flat to the floor. After a moment he cautiously raised his head again and looked out.

'Hello the house,' he heard a voice call softly.

'Who're you?' Lorrimar hissed.

'Arne, from the village. What's happening?'

'Wait,' Lorrimar thought for a moment. He remembered the military-looking owner of the Fenton Oak. He decided that there was very little chance the man was involved in Mannion's scheme. 'Do you know where the back door is?'

'Yes.'

'Get there, fast,' Lorrimar said and hastily turned to the door that opened directly into the kitchen and called to McKendrick. 'Bill, open the door, someone coming. Watch him until we're sure he's okay.'

'Right.' Lorrimar turned back to the window and checked the garden. The black shape had gone and he could see nothing else that moved.

He heard the sound of the kitchen door opening. He crossed the room and looked into the kitchen.

'Arne?'

'Yes.'

'Come in here,' Lorrimar said.

'He's a walking bloody arsenal,' McKendrick said.

'Leave everything there,' Lorrimar told Arne. He waited until the older man had laid down the two rifles he carried and fished a revolver from his pocket. Back in the breakfast-room Lorrimar guided Arne to the window and resumed his own position. 'What happened out there?' he asked.

'There are two men, both dead, they killed each other. One is . . .' Arne stopped, his eyes, accustomed to the darkness outside, had not taken long to re-adjust to the darker room. 'You're Lorrimar,' he said.

'Yes. Never mind that now. Carry on.'

'Two men. One tall, came from over here, near the house. He was shot from out towards the front of the house. The other man came from the same direction. Presumably to see who he had hit and finish him off. They both fired together.'

'And they're both dead?'

'Yes.'

'Christ.'

'The first man. He was with you?'

'Yes.'

'The other man, he was Japanese. He was wearing army-style clothing.'

'Yes.'

'For God's sake Lorrimar, what is happening here?'

'In a moment. Did you see anyone else out there?'

'No, but I heard a whistle. The Japanese had another man backing him up.'

'The other shooting, earlier, what was that?'

'The first long burst I don't know. We heard it as we went out to investigate the helicopters.'

'We?'

'The local policeman and me. We were not together. I stayed back to collect my shot gun. Just by the farm, opposite the church, there were two more men, dressed the same as the one out there. They killed the policeman.'

'Were they Japs?'

'I didn't see them close enough, but the others were.'

'What others?'

'I tried to get out of the village by car. They had the road blocked. Two of them, Japanese again. I went through the woods to the other road and there were two more, I think the same two who shot Constable Blake. They have that road blocked as well. That's when I decided to come up here and find out what is going on.' Arne paused. 'There was someone else, at the

Oak. An old man. He was staying for a few days. He had a gun, that revolver I brought with me. I killed him.'

'Was he Japanese?'

'No, English. He had a London accent. He was using the name Sidney Carver.'

'Sid Carver.' Lorrimar looked across the room to where Mannion was sitting. 'Hear that Ken? Your old mate's bought it. Now maybe you're starting to see the error of your ways.' He turned back to Arne. 'Okay, Mr. Arne we've got problems. I won't waste time telling you what we're doing here. What matters now is that there are people out there who want to be in here. You've just confirmed that they are Japanese. We don't know how many, but you've accounted for the whereabouts of six of them. It's likely there will be at least another six. We've got to hold them off until the police get here. Or the army.'

'They're on their way?'

'Bound to be.'

'My telephone went dead when I was talking to Scotland Yard.'

'The Yard. You talked to them?'

'Yes, Blake was in touch with them. Someone called Mason.'

'Arthur Mason, how did he get involved?'

'I don't know, he called Blake and told him there was trouble at the Hall.'

'They must have got wind of us sooner than

190

we thought. Still that's all to the good now.'

'Why the army Lorrimar? You still haven't told me what is happening.'

'They're after someone.' Lorrimar pointed upwards. 'He's upstairs, you'd better go and see for yourself, you won't believe me otherwise.' Arne went out into the hallway and Lorrimar called out to McKendrick.

'Bill, Jim's dead. I think we can trust Arne. When he comes downstairs, give him back his guns. Then we'd better have a rethink. Seems the opposition have the village sealed off, even when the law gets here they're going to have their work cut out getting in to us. Once the army are on the job things might move a bit faster because they'll have more fire-power, but that might take time and, until then, we could have a fight on our hands.'

'Okay Dave. You taking charge again?'

'I'm thinking about letting Arne do that.'

'Him?'

'Yes. I let Jim take over because this is his kind of game, not mine. Now he's dead this still isn't my kind of deal. Arne is ex-army, he might think their way.'

'Up to you mate, I'll go along with whatever you say.'

'Right. Martin, you hear that?'

'Yes.'

'What do you think?'

'Sounds like a good idea. I'll go along.' Arne

reappeared at the dining-room door and walked briskly down to Lorrimar.

'You're right,' he said. 'I wouldn't have believed you. What are your plans?'

'At the moment there aren't any. Jim, the one you saw get killed. He was in charge. This kind of fighting is his . . . was his line of work.'

'Well he wasn't very good at it if that's the case,' Arne said brusquely. 'For one thing if he was the only man with experience of this kind of fighting he should not have put himself at risk. For another you're not occupying the best part of the house. I'm not even sure you should be in the house.'

'Okay, Arne. Stop the sermons. You know as much as we all know now. From here on you give the orders. You should be good at it.'

'Are you serious Lorrimar?'

'Christ, this isn't the time for jokes. Of course I'm serious. Fighting a bunch of terrorists isn't my line of work and it isn't Bill's either, but we can both use guns.'

'Who is that?' Arne asked pointing to Martin.

'The Prince's bodyguard.'

'Sir James?'

'Sitting-room, across the hall.'

'The women?'

'Cloakroom. No windows.'

'None at all?'

'No. It opens into a small lavatory. There's a window in there, but it's small and anyone trying to get in won't be able to come in fast.'

'Very well.'

'So what do we do?'

'Any other weapons apart from those you all have?'

'Hand grenades.'

'Grenades? What were you planning on doing here Lorrimar?'

'Never mind that. What do you think we should do?'

'I'm not happy about staying in the house at all, but until we know exactly what is happening outside we'd better stay put. We're too thinly spread out. We'll reposition so we have the front of the house protected from downstairs. We'll have four men here, two at each of the front windows. The remaining two men and the women all upstairs at the rear of the house. Are there enough guns for Lady Garroway and the older girl?'

'Yes.'

'Okay, that's the way we'll play it for now. Then I'll want a volunteer to scout the area, do what your friend was trying to do. When we know the position outside we can decide whether to stay here or not.'

'I'll do it.'

'Good. Let's get everyone re-organised. Leave the man in the kitchen for the moment and the two by the front windows. We'll take the women upstairs and find the most secure place there.' Arne moved down the room. As he passed Mannion he looked round at Lorrimar. 'Who is he?'

'He started as one of us. Now he's joined the enemy. Given the right set of circumstances I reckon he might very well change sides again.'

'Like that? He's best left tied up then.' The two men went out into the hallway and Lorrimar led the way to the cloakroom. He opened the door and called out. There was no answer. He pushed the door wider and stepped inside. The cloakroom was empty. With his gun in hand he cautiously prodded open the door to the lavatory. The small window was open and there was a cold wind blowing into his face. The room was empty.

CHAPTER TWENTY-TWO

'But can we be certain?' Lady Garroway asked her eldest daughter.

'No, but it seems more likely doesn't it?'

'I don't know.'

'Think, Mother. Is it likely a gang of terrorists are here in the middle of Buckinghamshire?'

'This morning I wouldn't have thought it likely that a gang of violent criminals would come in here and imprison us in our own home.'

'Perhaps not,' Sarah Garroway said impatiently, 'but they did ...'

'So if that has happened, why couldn't the other be true as well?'

'Because it was obvious these men didn't know about ... they didn't know he would be here. When they found out they panicked. Now they're in a trap of their own making. They can't get out without father's money or the aircraft and the helicopter they want. And they can't risk staying here because they know there will soon be every policeman for miles around looking for the Prince.'

'So why have they told us there are terrorists outside?'

'Two reasons. One to keep us all quiet. The other to give them an appearance of being loyal and patriotic heroes. So that when they are caught they will be able to ask for leniency.'

'But if there aren't any terrorists outside how will they do that?'

'Because we're all assuming there are. We would say we thought there was someone out there.'

'But ...'

'I think we should get out now. The window in there, it's small but none of us is very big. We can all get through it and go for help. At least it will reduce the number of hostages the gang has.'

'But supposing there are terrorists out there?'

'There won't be.'

'But suppose there are?' Lady Garroway insisted.

'If there are, it's dark. We know the grounds better than they do. We can get away.'

'I don't know Sarah.'

'Well I'm going.' The young woman opened the door between the cloakroom and the lavatory. Cautiously she reached up and opened the window. Then she climbed up onto the lavatory seat and then on to the top of the cistern. She pushed the window fully open and looked out. She turned to her mother. 'Well?' she asked.

'Oh, we should stay together Sarah.'

'I agree, but outside, not in.'

'Alright. Get through the window, I'll help Belinda through.' It was several minutes before they were all outside. Sarah Garroway reached out and took her sister by the hand. Then the three of them began to cross the gravel pathway that surrounded the Hall. They reached the grass at the far side of the path and Sarah moved to her left until she could see the end of the footpath that led down to Remenham Lane. With her sister and her mother behind her she began to walk quickly down the sloping, muddy path. They were almost one hundred yards from the house and already into the woods when a man stepped out from the trees. Sarah stopped abruptly and turned back. Behind her, Belinda and Lady Garroway had stopped too. Sarah could see from their expressions that they had not yet seen the man. Sarah started to speak and then, behind her mother, she saw another man step out from the trees. She turned back again and looked at the first man in the darkness. He was dressed in a uniform of sorts and he was carrying a gun, a gun that was levelled at her. She looked up into his face.

'I'm sorry Mother,' she said softly. 'I was wrong.'

The two men took them back up the path until they reached the edge of the trees and then they struck off across the sloping lawns, keeping close to the tree line until they were almost at the Pearson's cottage. Two more men appeared out of the darkness and the first two turned and went back the way they had come. The small procession continued on up to the cottage.

'Inside please ladies,' one of the two men said. Sarah could not detect any accent in the man's voice, but, as she stepped past him, she could see that, like the first two men, he too was Japanese. Inside, the cottage was in darkness and she had to lead her sister and her mother uncertainly through the unfamiliar rooms. When they were in what she took to be the Pearson's dining-room she heard the man speak again, this time in his own language and his companion answered and then went out.

'Where are Mr. and Mrs. Pearson?' Sarah

asked.

'They are upstairs. They will come to no harm, no more than any of you, provided that you all do exactly as I tell you.' He crossed the room and switched on a small table lamp. In its light she could see that the man was tall and young. His face held no expression at all.

'What are. . . ?' Sarah began to speak but the tall man interrupted her.

'No questions. You are not entitled to ask any. Here,' he tossed a coil of white rope to her. She caught it, her action involuntary. The rope was hard to the touch, nylon not hemp. 'Tie up your mother. Do it well.'

'I . . .' The man stepped forward and slapped her hard across the face, the crack of his hand on her flesh sharp in the silence.

'Say nothing more. Next time it will be your sister.' The pain from the slap began to sting and Sarah felt tears form in her eyes as she turned to her mother. She tied Lady Garroway's hands behind her and then looked at the man. 'Sit in that chair,' he said to the older woman. 'Now, tie her ankles and then tie her to the chair.' There was silence in the room and then, softly, the youngest girl began to weep. The man ignored her. When Sarah was finished he looked at Belinda. 'Be quiet,' he said. 'You will now tie your sister's hands in the same way.' He waited until Belinda had done as he had ordered and then he crossed to where Sarah stood and nodded at another chair. She sat down and he laid his gun on the table and quickly tied her securely to the chair. Then he tied up the young girl and then stood back and looked at them. 'I will not gag you,' he said quietly. 'But I will warn you once only. Apart from us there is no one to hear and if we hear you, we shall punish you. Is that understood?' He paused and then crossed the room and turned out the light. Moments later he went through the door and closed it quietly behind him. In the room the only sound was the sobbing of Belinda Garroway. After a moment her mother began to speak softly to her and eventually the crying stopped. Sarah Garroway did not speak at all.

CHAPTER TWENTY-THREE

There was no sign that anyone had been near the two helicopters when Webb and Manning approached them. Webb gestured at the nearest of the two machines.

'You take this one, I'll take the far one. Climb inside, put a burst into the control panel then get out and put a second burst in the fuel tanks. Then we move fast. Across to the church.' Webb turned away and ran to the second helicopter. As he climbed on board he heard a burst of firing behind him and seconds later he fired a burst from the dead man's automatic rifle into the control panel of the helicopter. He scrambled back to the door and jumped down to the ground. He steadied himself and fired into the fuel tanks. He turned and saw Manning coming across the grass towards him. The two men sprinted to the church. Close by the building they stopped.

'Okay?' Webb asked.

'Yes sir. I thought they'd go up in flames.'

'Doesn't matter, with the instruments smashed and the fuel tanks holed they're grounded.'

'What now sir?'

'We ought to find some way of making contact with someone. You go back to that village where we left the main road. Don't get involved with anyone if you can help it. Keep out of sight until you can find a car and get to a telephone that works.'

'Yes sir. What are you going to do?'

'I'll make a quick tour of the village, see what I can find out. We still don't know who we're up against, or why. Get moving then.' Webb stayed where he was, watching until the rifleman disappeared from his sight. Then he ran round to the front of the church and tried the door. It was unlocked. Inside, the building was empty. He ran steadily down the track that led from the church to the road. Directly opposite was a farm and he could see several people in the garden.

As far as he could make out in the light that streamed from the windows of the house they were all civilians. He crossed the road cautiously and looked over the wall. There were four people, two men and two women. Lying on the ground was a third man, he was wearing a uniform. Webb leaned over the wall and sighted the AK 47.

'Nobody move,' he said. He moved sideways along the wall until he reached the gate and went through it. 'What happened?' he asked.

'This is Mr. Blake, he's the policeman. Somebody's shot him.' The speaker was one of the two men.

'Who shot him?' Webb asked.

'Don't know. I think it was somebody who came out of them helicopters,' the man said. Webb glanced at the house. He pointed at one of the women.

'Go inside and switch off all the lights,' he ordered. 'You're all targets out here.' He waited until the woman did as he had said and then stepped further into the garden. As he approached the two men he saw that the one who had remained silent was holding a shotgun. 'Break it open,' he said. The man did as he was told. 'You'd better get inside,' he said. 'Keep away from the windows.' He turned away, hesitated and turned back. 'Keep that shotgun by you, but be sure who you're shooting at before you use it.'

'Who are they?' the first man asked.

'No idea, but they look Chinese.'

'Chinese? Bloody hell, have we been invaded?' Webb had difficulty in not smiling.

'No,' he said. 'Just keep out of sight. No heroics. Okay?'

'Don't worry about that,' the man said.

'There was other shooting,' the first man said.

'Those up the road earlier?'

'Yes and again a few minutes ago by the church.'

'I know about them.'

'There was one from the pub. Sounded like a shotgun. Then we heard a car come out of the car park at the back of the pub—went up the road.'

'Right,' said Webb. 'I'll have a look. Oh, is your telephone working?'

'No. We tried to call the police.' Webb nodded and went out of the gate and jog-trotted down the road towards where the man had indicated the village pub lay.

Rifleman Manning saw the two men lying in a small depression by the roadside a few yards from a newly erected barricade. Beyond the barricade he could see the burnt-out remains of the Landrover. He looked carefully around him but he could see no sign of movement. The men were both on the opposite side of the road to where he stood and he was confident that he could pass without detection. He hesitated. The

202

smell from the wreckage of the vehicle drifted into his nostrils and he tightened his grip on the SLR. Then he slowly relaxed, realising that his orders to bring help were the best, the only course of action he could follow. He began to move ahead again, noting that the farm buildings, close to where the two men lay were in darkness. He wondered fleetingly if the occupants had suffered the same fate as McIntosh and Lowe. He was well past the road block and had begun to pick up his pace once more when he saw the car swung sideways across the road. He moved on more slowly and was almost upon the man standing motionless in the hedgerow before he saw him. The man was dressed in ordinary civilian clothes but there was a revolver in his gloved hands. Manning considered the position the man stood in. Clearly the car had approached from the south and the man was facing towards the village. Facing towards the first barricade he had seen. He decided there was a possibility that the man was not on the same side as the others. Whether that put him on his side was another matter, but he decided it was worth the risk. He eased forward out of the darkness and pressed the muzzle of his rifle into the man's body.

CHAPTER TWENTY-FOUR

Okada Kurusu did not look the way Lorrimar had assumed he would. Tall, only fractionally below Lorrimar's five feet ten inches, he was slim but looked heavier than he probably was, the loose camouflaged combat suit giving an illusion of heavy-build. His face was thin and there was no humour in the eyes and the mouth was a severe line that looked as if it rarely, if ever, smiled. He was unarmed. The two men stood facing each other in the hallway of the house. All the doors into the rooms off the hallway were closed. Lorrimar and Arne had decided that although the terrorists knew about everyone in the house with the sole exception of Arne, there was little point in giving away information. Arne and the Prince were on the first floor with Sergeant Martin, the Prince's bodyguard. McKendrick was still in the kitchen and Sir James Garroway had crossed into the dining-room. Mannion was trussed and gagged and wedged into the laundry room off the kitchen. Lorrimar had experienced a few desperate moments with Garroway when the financier had learned of the disappearance of his wife and daughters, but he had rapidly recovered and accepted that there was no time for recriminations. Lorrimar eyed the tall

Japanese carefully.

'We'll go in here,' he said, pointing to the sitting-room door.

'As you wish,' Kurusu said. The two men went into the room, Kurusu first with Lorrimar following several paces behind.

'Well?' Lorrimar asked.

'I think we have a temporary stalemate Mr. Lorrimar,' the terrorist said. There was no trace of accent in his voice, if anything he spoke better English than most of Lorrimar's associates.

For the tall Japanese the sudden appearance of the two women and the young girl had handed him an unexpected advantage. It was an advantage he needed although he had not expected he would need it. When the raid had been planned almost every conceivable contingency had been covered. The original idea had been to move a detachment of men, slowly assembled in England over the preceding six months, and attack at RAF station. There they would steal two helicopters and then move on to Fenton to kidnap the Prince with no outside help being used. Kurusu had been one of those who had vetoed that particular part of the plan. He had argued that if anything went wrong, anything that was beyond their control; if the Prince failed to attend the dinner; if the dinner was cancelled; if he decided against picking up the Garroway girl *en route*; if their informant at the Palace failed to maintain his previous high standard of information; if anything prevented the attack taking place after they had raided the RAF station, then a second attempt at a later date would be that much more difficult.

That was when he had suggested they hire a team of London criminals to make the preliminary moves, their own assault on the RAF station being delayed until they had word that the Hall had been secured and that the Prince was on his way to keep his engagement. That way, he had reasoned, if anything went wrong they would be able to try again. Once the principle was agreed it had been relatively easy to find Mannion and persuade him to co-operate on a scheme that would end in the betrayal of his colleagues. Kurusu had total contempt for Mannion's greed. His own motivation was simple and, to him, pure. Together with his companions he sought a world that knew no government, no establishment, no law. Total freedom for the individual to take what he wanted, when, and by whatever methods he chose. He had already applied that creed since joining the group and as a result had killed seventeen men and three women. He expected that number to increase before the present affair was over. He meant to have the hostage he wanted. The leverage the kidnapped Prince would give him and his group over the British government was incalculable. The group had reasoned that the effect would be greater than would result from the kidnapping of an elected head of state. He would have liked to have tried for the Monarch, but realism was one of his better traits. He knew that the relatively casual manner in which the British protected the members of their Royal Family, apart from the Monarch and the heir, was ideal for their purposes. Too much protection meant too much force in an attack and the object of this particular exercise was not to kill, but to kidnap.

He looked at Lorrimar. He had not expected too much opposition. He glanced at his watch. He wanted the Prince in his hands and the entire position consolidated, by dawn at the latest. He knew that his back-up group would be able to mislead the RAF for a while. They had taken four helicopters in a sudden, vicious and bloody attack. Two machines, each with only a pilot on board had made a high-level run from the station giving radar operators an easily seen trace on their screens. The two machines carrying the main force had made a low-level run directly to the field in Fenton village. So far there was good reason to hope that their attempt to confuse the military was succeeding.

He had needed to get into the Hall and find out why Mannion had not let them in, why he had not dealt with the small matter of eliminating his three companions. Finding the three women in the grounds had given him the way into the Hall. When he had hailed the house and told them he wanted to talk he had not been too surprised when Lorrimar, not Mannion, had answered and called him in. His mind flickered over the possible ways to remove the men in the house. There was no doubt in his mind that a swift violent end would be the best, but there was an element of risk to the Prince. He wondered if Lorrimar would be prepared to deal.

'A stalemate?' Lorrimar asked. 'That's what you think we have is it?'

'Of course we have, let us not play games. You were set up, with the aid of your friend Mannion.'

'Your friend, not mine.'

'Then he has no friends. His usefulness to us is over.'

'I thought it might be.'

'A clever man, but a greedy one. Greed can overcome most things.'

'Get on with it.'

'Ah, you are not interested in a philosophical discussion. Quite right. Very well, we expected an easier operation than this. Mannion was supposed to come out and allow some of us into the house to take His Royal Highness. When Mannion did not appear we assumed, correctly as it turned out, that you had suspected all was not as it should be with regard to Mannion's part in the affair. That meant that you might well suspect our presence, or have even been

208

told by Mannion. I imagine he would talk readily under pressure.'

'Get to the point.'

'The point, Mr. Lorrimar, is that we have the three women. We want the Prince. We will exchange them for him. No one dies.'

'Two are dead already.'

'Your man Hart. Yes and one of our men too. How did you know that Mr. Lorrimar? No one else has been outside.' Lorrimar thought quickly.

'We heard the firing. Jim didn't come back.'

'Still you ... never mind. You have heard our proposal.'

'What do you want him for?'

'Really, Mr Lorrimar, what better hostage could we have? Any demand we make, anything at all and it will be ours.'

'You think so?'

'Don't you?'

'And you expect us to hand him over?'

'Why not? You are not a servant of the government, you are not a soldier, you are not a patriot, you are a criminal. Your every action is against the establishment. You are an enemy of the state. Why should you not do so?' Lorrimar grinned humourlessly at the Japanese.

'Why not? Because you haven't mentioned the price yet.' Kurusu nodded his head slowly.

'Of course. Forgive me. An offer was made to Mannion . . .'

'Another four million. Don't make the mistake of assuming I will think like him.'

'Of course not. Four million was a ridiculous figure.'

'Was it?'

'Of course, we do not have ... ah, you are thinking of the original sum, that which was to come from Sir James. Was he co-operating?'

'Yes.'

'And you think he would have produced the money?'

'Yes.'

'You have a deal in mind I think Mr. Lorrimar.'

'Yes. By now the police must know that the Prince is missing. It won't take them long to track him here. They will try to contact his bodyguard and when they find they can't get a reply they'll descend on Fenton in their hundreds. In fact they're probably on their way now.'

'They will not get here. The village is isolated. Roadblocks on all three roads in. We can keep them out for long enough to do what we have to do.'

'What if they bring in the army? Can you hold them off?'

'In small numbers, obviously if they make a general assault we will be in difficulties, but so long as we have His Royal Highness they are unlikely to do anything too aggressive.'

'So, how long can you hold out here?'

Lorrimar asked.

'Here?'

'In the Hall.'

'With you?'

'Yes. We hold the Hall together and stay put until Monday. Then we collect the four million Garroway is raising, he gets his family back and we all go out in your helicopters. Your men, Mannion and McKendrick and the Prince.'

'Mannion?'

'He stays with us because he knows where we're going. I don't want the police cutting off our line of retreat.'

'Where do we take you?'

'To the airfield at Abingdon.'

'As your original plan?'

'Yes.' Kurusu studied Lorrimar's face.

'You will do that? Co-operate with us in the defence of this building?'

'Yes.'

'What about the others?'

'They'll agree, those that don't will have no alternative.'

'I am not sure about the timing Mr. Lorrimar. I had planned on being out of here rather sooner than Monday.'

'It could be worth waiting for.'

'Perhaps. I will discuss it with my colleagues.' Kurusu stood up and crossed to the door. Lorrimar followed and watched carefully as he opened the main door. The tall Japanese

211

stepped out into the darkness and closed the door behind him. Lorrimar switched out the lights in the sitting-room and in the hallway and hurried to the foot of the stairs.

'Arne,' he called softly. He heard a door open above.

'Yes?'

'Down here. Fast.' The older man came down to where Lorrimar waited.

'Well?'

'As we expected. He wanted to trade. The women for him.'

'And?'

'I've stalled him. I've suggested a deal. We help him defend the Hall against the police and the army until Monday and then we collect the original ransom and we all go out together.'

'What original ransom?'

'What ... oh, yes, sorry you don't know about that.' Lorrimar quickly told Arne of the reason they were all there. 'I'm not sure if he is going to buy it, but the chances are he will pretend to. If he does that will necessitate him bringing some men inside the house. They don't know about you so we have an edge. You and the hand grenades. If we can take out the men he sends in, then we will have a chance to get out and take care of the rest of them.'

'Whatever happens you're going to be in a lot of trouble.'

'I expect I am.'

'Did you get any idea how many men there are?'

'He said there are three road blocks. You've seen two of them and there were two men at each. If there are two at the third then that makes six men. There were probably about sixteen to begin with. That leaves ten available to surround the house. We know one is dead, that leaves nine.'

'There is probably one man at least guarding the helicopters.'

'Leaving eight.'

'Okay. Let's see what happens when . . . if he comes back to continue talking.'

'In the meantime what are we doing? We can't take a chance on letting them sneak in on us like they did before.'

'If that is what happened.'

'What?'

'Maybe the women left and were captured.'

'Maybe. Anyway, what do we do now?'

'We need at least two men with the Prince at all times.'

'We'll put Sir James up there.'

'Why?'

'He doesn't know we're pretending to barter with his family's life.'

'I don't think it will make a difference if he does.'

'I don't want to take that chance. If we put him up there he won't be able to hear what's going on down here.'

'He'll probably guess. He's not a fool.'

'Maybe.'

'Very well.' Arne said. 'Send him up then.' Lorrimar went down the hallway to the dining-room door and called to Garroway and told him what was wanted.

'What did their man say about my wife and daughters?' Garroway asked.

'They're unharmed,' Lorrimar said realising that it had not occurred to him to ask Kurusu about the women.

'They want an exchange I suppose,' Garroway said. Lorrimar glanced at Arne who had followed him from the stairs.

'That's very likely what they want.'

'What have you said?'

'We're stalling him.' Lorimar abruptly decided there was nothing to be gained by attempting to deceive the financier. He repeated the conversation he had had with the terrorist and with Arne.

'You're taking risks with many lives,' Garroway said, 'Both of you. I trust your judgement Mr. Arne. I know of your record in the army, but you,' he looked at Lorrimar. 'In the circumstances I cannot trust you at all. Without you none of this would have . . .'

'Yes . . .' Lorrimar interrupted, but Garroway ignored him.

' . . . happened. Whatever the outcome I shall

regard you and your colleagues as wholly responsible.' He hefted the rifle he carried. 'If my wife or my daughters are killed then I will do my very best to kill you.' Lorrimar grinned at the other man, but there was no amusement in his eyes.

'Let's wait and see. Now, upstairs. Keep the Prince in your sight at all times. No need to tell Martin the same. He won't leave his side now. Keep him away from the windows, but you and Martin maintain a close watch on the grounds. Sing out if you see any movement.' Garroway nodded and walked away towards the stairs. Lorrimar looked at Arne. 'I haven't made a friend there,' he remarked.

'For God's sake Lorrimar,' Arne said bitterly. 'What do you expect? You forced your way in here at gunpoint, threatened his wife and daughters and now, as a direct result, the lives of everyone in the house and probably in the entire village are at risk. Four men are already dead, more probably, from the firing we heard earlier. Of course he doesn't like you. And while we're talking this way let me assure you that if his wife or his daughters are killed, and if he doesn't kill you, then I will.' Lorrimar looked at Arne carefully.

'Okay Arne,' he said. 'Let's knock it off shall we. Like it or not we're on the same side now. Cut out all the who'll kill who stuff. Because if it does come to that you needn't think I shall be standing around waiting for either of you to take potshots at me.' The two men stood glaring at each other. Arne was the first to speak.

'Very well. Let's concentrate on keeping ourselves and everyone else alive. Where do you think they're holding the women?'

'Can't say. A likely place will be the cottage where the housekeeper lives. It's close and I don't think they have the strength to spread men over too great an area. They're under strength already with six men on the road blocks, so the chances are they will want everyone close at hand.'

'You're probably right,' Arne said thoughtfully.

'Where does that leave us?' asked Lorrimar.

'It leaves us needing to know more about what is happening outside. It also means we need to get word out to whoever is trying to get in to help us.'

'We can't do that, unless someone makes a run for it. Pity we . . .'

'Damn it,' Arne said softly.

'What?'

'Blake's Landrover. It's in my garage.'

'The policeman?'

'Yes. He put it in there to keep it out of sight. It has a radio.'

'Can we get to it?'

'I got here so I suppose someone can get back.'

'Wait a minute.' Lorrimar said. 'Let's take it a step at a time. First we don't know that Kurusu is going to play ball with me. If he comes back with a deal that brings some of his men into the house then we need everyone here. Second, if he doesn't come back with a deal then it will mean an all out attack from them. If that happens we still need everyone here. Anyway I'm not sure there's a lot to be gained by telling the people outside what is going on, they must have a pretty good idea by now.'

'That isn't the main reason for going out, it's important that we find out what we are faced with here.'

'We know what we're faced with.'

'We don't know their positions, we don't know their strength, we don't even know that the women are alive.'

'You think they might have killed them?'

'It's not impossible.'

'Okay, but it can't be you that goes out. I'm not going to ask Bill. Martin won't leave the Prince so that leaves me.'

'And you can't go until we know whether or not Kurusu is coming back to talk to you.'

'We can't wait too long. Another few hours and it will be daylight.'

'Yes,' Arne nodded his head in agreement. He paused before continuing. 'If I was out there I don't think I would be too worried about whether or not I had the Prince.'

'Why not?'

'If they have explosives, grenades, small bombs, light artillery, all of which is highly likely, then they have a great deal of strength just staying where they are. If a relief force attempts to take them, all they have to do is threaten to turn their fire-power onto this building and kill everyone in it.'

'They would sign their own death warrants if they did that.'

'That might not be of much consequence to them.'

'Kurusu didn't look like a fanatic.'

'He has to be one, to be here.'

'I expect you're right,' Lorrimar said. 'Okay, what do we do now?'

'Wait. But I agree with you we should set a time limit. If we haven't heard from Kurusu by an hour before dawn then someone should go out and attempt a survey of their positions and attempt to locate Lady Garroway and her daughters.'

'Right, an hour before dawn it is.' Lorrimar glanced at his watch. 'I think we should take turns to try to get some sleep. An hour each, it will help.'

'Good idea, you'd better go first, seeing you'll be going outside. You'll need to be as alert as possible.' Lorrimar nodded his head.

'Okay. I'll take the settee in the sitting-room.' He walked through to the other room and stretched out on the settee. He closed his eyes and tried to relax his mind. He had no intention of sleeping. Despite their circumstances there were still too many people in the house who were his natural enemies to warrant taking a risk. He had been lying there for less than twenty minutes when there was a short burst of automatic rifle fire. The bullets smashed into the heavy front door of the house. Kurusu had apparently decided not to do a deal.

In fact he had seriously considered launching a frontal assault on the house but then, still unwilling to risk harming the man they hoped to kidnap, he had decided on an attempt to draw at least some of the fire power from the Hall by giving the men inside a reason to come out. With the Pearsons securely bound in an upstairs room he took Lady Garroway and her daughters out of the cottage. He and the man he had with him took care to make sufficient noise as they were leaving to ensure that the Pearsons heard them go. He hoped the couple would then attempt to make the men at the Hall hear them. If that didn't work he had already decided on a plan to draw Lorrimar out. After a few moments' thought he had settled on the church as a convenient and safe place to hold the women. The location was one that gave him a better chance to effect an ambush. The church stood on raised ground at the end of a long, wide footpath that led from the road. The churchyard was well-kept, all derelict graves had long since been tidied and now, apart from a few close to the church walls, they were covered with simple flat stones. There were some tree clumps but they were well clear of the building and would not provide adequate cover for an attacking force. The church seemed to be an excellent place for him.

CHAPTER TWENTY-FIVE

The information Rifleman Manning of the Royal Green Jackets was able to supply to Detective Chief Superintendent Arthur Mason was helpful but inconclusive. Apart from the one encouraging fact that the destruction of the helicopters had effectively blocked an escape route, all that he really had were more unanswered questions that he had had before. Guarded messages came over the radio and confirmed that the other police cars had sealed the roads leading out of Fenton to the north. They also conveyed the information that the roads were barricaded to prevent access to the village.

'It doesn't help a lot,' he said quietly, more to himself than to the soldier.

'Sir?'

'Eh? Oh, just thinking aloud. They can't get

out by air or road. But you came out easily enough so there's nothing to prevent them from doing the same thing.'

'Yes, but if I came out I can go back and take you with me.' Mason looked at him speculatively.

'I'm not sure that's what we're best equipped to do. We're not dressed for it and more important we're not adequately armed. I think it will be best if we wait for the army.'

'I am army,' Manning said. 'And so's Lieutenant Webb and he's still in there. If you're sure help is on its way then there's no reason for me to stay here. I'll go back and join him.' Mason looked at him carefully.

'I have no real authority over you son, but it might be as well if you stayed outside.'

'No, you're going to need someone inside and the Lieutenant can't cope on his own.'

'Okay, but be careful and try to find some way of getting word back to us about their strength and more important who's doing what in there.'

'As far as I'm concerned anyone except the people that live here are the enemy.'

'Don't jump to conclusions. The men I told you about might not be directly involved with...'

'I'm not going to risk my life on a guess,' Manning interrupted. 'If they're in there for the reason you told me then they're more likely to be on the other side than on mine.'

'You might need their help, remember, don't jump to conclusions.'

'Yes, well, maybe,' Manning said. 'I'm off then.'

'Okay, be careful,' Mason said and watched as the young soldier turned and walked quietly into the woods that bordered the road. In seconds he had disappeared from sight. Mason turned as he heard the sound of someone approaching on foot. He recognised the police officer Inspector Jackson had been told to drop off in Lower Assendon.

'Well?' he asked.

'Telephones there are working sir. I used one at a house on the corner of the road. I've called the Yard and the local nick. No developments except that the local Task Force are up to their eyes in an emergency. The RAF have lost four helicopters and several men have been killed. Sounds like a terrorist raid and not far from here.'

'Get on the radio. Tell them we've found their helicopters, or at least some of them and we can't wait much longer.'

'Yes sir.'

'Good man. I'm getting impatient with all this hanging about. And cold.' Mason looked into the woods where Manning had gone. For a moment he wondered briefly if he had done the right thing in letting him go back alone. Then

222

he shrugged, with any amount of luck they would be following him soon.

Manning was within a hundred yards of the field where the helicopters lay crippled when he decided to cross the road and see if he could see any signs of activity at the Hall. The story the senior police officer had told him had seemed fantastic at first but, as he thought more about it, he had realised that only something as extraordinary as an attempt to kidnap a member of the Royal Family could account for the unprovoked attack on the Landrover. The sight of a totally unexpected army vehicle must have panicked the men at the barricade. He crossed the road and climbed through a wire fence and crawled into the shrubbery that bordered the driveway entrance to the house. He eased his way forward until he was at the edge of a long rising sweep of lawn. In the blackness he could not make out the house. There were no lights and no sounds or movements. He had decided to move on, back towards the village in an attempt to regain contact with the lieutenant when he heard a sound to his right. He froze in his position and waited. After a moment he heard the noise again. Several people were coming towards the road. They were walking on the grass beside the drive but their precaution against too much noise was not enough. He brought up the SLR and waited, then the cautioning of the policeman came into mind.

There was a possibility that they were not allied to the group who had attacked the Landrover. At that moment one of the group of vague, shadowy figures stumbled, fell and cried out. It was a woman's voice. Manning lowered the SLR and breathed a sigh of relief that he had waited. The group passed from his sight and after a few moments he crawled back into the shrubbery and made his way to the roadside. The group passed him as he lay on the wet ground. He counted five, two men, one leading and one following, and three women. One of the women was small and appeared to Manning to be little more than a girl. He tracked them as they skirted the field where the helicopters stood and he tensed, expecting the worst when they found the dead body of the man left to guard the machines. The group did not pause, but passed the field and turned into the lane that led up to the church. He followed cautiously and watched as the five figures went into the church. Moments later the two men came out again and stood talking. Manning was too far away to hear what was said but then one figure, the taller of the two men, turned away and moved back down the path towards where Manning lay hidden. The rifleman rapidly considered the options open to him and decided that there were unlikely to be many opportunities to find the enemy when they were not grouped together. He came to his feet and stepped out into the path, levelling the SLR at the man coming towards him. The man stopped.

'Lay down the gun,' Manning said and in silence the man did so. 'Now step over it and come closer, slowly.' The man did as he was commanded. Manning moved forward carefully. Then, suddenly, he heard a sound behind him, he began to turn and then he felt a blow in the middle of his back, not a hard blow, almost as if a friend had come up and slapped him in greeting. He tried to continue the turn but there was suddenly no strength in his muscles and he felt his legs begin to buckle. Then, from the place where he had felt the blow, there came a biting, unbearable pain and he realised that the hand that had delivered the blow had held a knife. He had been stabbed. He felt the SLR slip from his fingers and then clatter onto the ground, seconds later he fell over it. He was dimly aware that someone had knelt beside him. He felt his head being lifted and turned. A hand pulled away the collar of his jacket and he felt the cold air on his throat. Then he felt a colder, icier touch against his throat that turned to pressure, then turned to pain. He felt his blood rush to meet the air that was trying unavailingly, to reach his lungs.

After his colleague had cut the soldier's throat Kurusu helped drag the body off the pathway that led to the church. The fact that the soldier was alone reassured him slightly. He guessed

225

that the man had survived the attack on the Landrover and for the second time that night he cursed the unexpected arrival of the vehicle at the road junction just as they were preparing to barricade the road. It also angered him that his men had panicked and opened fire. There was little doubt in his mind that the appearance of the Landrover had been completely coincidental. Had they left them alone, they might well have moved off again. He sent the man with him to double up the guard at the church and he used a portable two-way radio to call in one man from each of the three road-blocks and the two men he had stationed along the footpath at the south-east corner of the Hall. They reported that their colleague, the man sent to destroy the telephone lines to the area, had not returned. Kurusu mentally wrote-off the man. He ordered the two men to move directly behind the house and when the other three men arrived he moved with them to a position within easy range of the Hall. Then he waited for a few minutes. When he was satisfied there was no sign or sound of movement he prepared to order the diversion he had planned to draw Lorrimar out.

★   ★   ★

Sarah Garroway finally managed to calm her mother. They had already agreed to avoid precipitating conflict with their captors and in the event it had not proved difficult. Apart from the tall leader of the group, none of the others had spoken in English, although she was certain that one of them did understand. She knew that any action or any words that might anger the terrorists should be avoided and her mother had agreed. Her young sister had remained remarkably calm. After her one bout of tears at the Pearsons' cottage she had recovered her detached, mature, attitude. Surprisingly it was Lady Garroway who began to shake uncontrollably shortly after they had been taken into the church and in trying to calm her Sarah had completely ignored Belinda. She was as surprised as the two guards when the little girl suddenly tried to escape from the building. One of the two men caught up with her by the door and seized her by the hair. The girl screamed once, sharply and clearly and then the man clasped his hand over her mouth and the sound was choked off. Sarah started to rise to her feet but the second man stepped forward, raising his automatic rifle. She sank back to the floor and watched helplessly as her sister was dragged back to their place in the centre of the church. The guard thrust the young girl from him and she fell, sprawling across the floor and lay there, sobbing.

'Belinda, it's alright. Don't cry darling, it will soon be over.' Sarah put her arms around her sister and held her tightly. Beside her she could feel Lady Garroway's trembling had stopped and after a moment she felt her mother's hand on her arm.

'I'll take her Sarah. Come, Belinda, your sister is right. Everything will soon be over.' Lady Garroway looked at her eldest daughter over the top of Belinda's blonde head. Her expression, indistinct in the darkness, implied that her thoughts told her differently. 'I'm sorry Sarah, my fault that Belinda did that. I should not have let myself go. It must have frightened her.'

'Perhaps...'

'Quiet.' One of the guards snapped out the order. There was silence and then from outside the church they heard the soft sound of voices. Sarah felt her hopes flare suddenly. The man who had spoken reached out a hand and pulled her roughly to her feet. 'You too,' he hissed at Lady Garroway. The two women stood uncertainly in the middle of the aisle, facing down towards the door. One of the guards was already moving down towards the door, crouched low and keeping close to the pew ends. The other man moved quietly away to the side of the church. Sarah stared at the main door, a darker shadow in the gloom at the end of the church beyond the high screen of wood and glass that stretched across the end of the centre aisle. There was total silence in the church.

CHAPTER TWENTY-SIX

Lorrimar stood motionless outside the kitchen door of the house. He moved his eyes carefully across from right to left and then back again. He could see no sign of any movement. He began to edge his way around the house, keeping close to the wall of the building. When he was at the far side of the garage he took a deep breath and moved out into the garden. He had decided, after talking to Arne, that he would rely on speed and surprise, that an attempt to use unfamiliar methods of movement, such as crawling along the ground, would be more likely to run him into trouble. Crouched low, he moved quickly across the grass, weaving slightly from side to side until he reached the long grass Arne had used for cover on the way in. He dropped to the ground and listened. He had both .44's with him, one in his hand and one in reserve. He had decided against taking a rifle but at Arne's insistence he had two grenades stuffed deep into the pockets of Arne's anorak. Certain there was no movement near to him he moved on again, pausing every twenty yards to listen and re-check his bearings. He saw and heard nothing until he was within sight of the Fenton Oak. Then he caught a glimpse of a movement directly between him and the inn.

He dropped to the ground and waited. The movement became identifiable as a man and Lorrimar brought up his Smith & Wesson and took careful aim, holding the gun two-handed, both forearms steadied on the ground. He registered that the man wore a uniform and he began to squeeze the trigger when the man saw him and froze to the spot. Lorrimar held the pressure on the trigger and waited. The man looked at him and in the darkness Lorrimar tried vainly to see his features.

'Say something,' Lorrimar said softly. 'And,' he added, 'your life depends on what you say.'

'My name is Webb,' the man said quietly. 'I am a lieutenant in the Royal Green Jackets and, by Christ, if you fire that thing you'd better make the first shot count because you won't get the chance of a second.' Lorrimar let out his breath slowly and relaxed pressure on the trigger. He let the barrel of the gun swing away to one side.

'Even better than the U.S. Cavalry,' he said.

Lorrimar's reappearance at the Hall with the lieutenant brought relief to everyone. Even the realisation that the young officer was alone did not entirely dispel the excitement. Webb, Arne and Lorrimar held a hasty discussion as soon as Webb had talked to the Prince. Webb was certain of the best move for the group at the Hall to make.

'Get out now, before it is light,' he said.

'The risk will be great, too great. I don't know that we can take that risk with His Royal Highness's life,' Arne protested.

'Yes we can, and with his approval.'

'You told him you wanted to do that?'

'Yes.'

'Well . . .'

'Look,' Webb said. 'At a rough estimate there are twelve or fourteen men out there. There are eight of us. The armaments we have here are adequate to give us the opportunity to provide cover on the move. They are not adequate to provide an effective defence of this house.'

'I don't know . . .' Arne began.

'I know you mean well Mr. Arne, but things have changed a bit since your day. These men we are dealing with are terrorists, I don't know exactly who or what they represent but they don't operate by the rules you knew.'

'Rules,' Arne said. 'Rules were very rarely in evidence in the last campaign I was in.'

'Maybe not, but there are differences.'

'I . . .' This time Lorrimar interrupted the older man.

'I think I agree with the lieutenant,' he said. 'We're on fairly good odds. It's not beyond possibility that Kurusu has found out what Webb has done to his helicopters. That will make him desperate to reach a quick solution. And don't forget he has Lady Garroway and her daughters. Wherever they are we are more likely to be able to help them from outside.' Arne hesitated for a moment and then he nodded his head.

'Very well,' he said. 'How do you propose going out?'

'The front of the house,' Webb said.

'The front?'

'Yes. There's a car outside the front, I saw it as we came up across the lawn.' Arne looked questioningly at Lorrimar.

'It's Garroway's Rolls,' Lorrimar said.

'Right, sorry it has to be a Rolls but it can't be helped. We set fire to it. Not where it is, we'll have to move it first. Then set it alight and wait for the bang when the petrol tank goes up.'

'Then what?'

'They will expect we're creating a diversion in order to get out of the back of the house. They will split their men. More round the back than the front. We go out at the front and the chances are we'll have no more than a couple of men between us and the road.'

'It only needs a stray bullet,' Arne said.

'That could happen here,' Webb said impatiently. 'If they attack the house nobody's safe.'

'And the Prince agrees?'

'Yes.'

'You told him exactly what you had in mind when you were upstairs?'

'Yes.'

'Where are we going? To get the radio?'

'No.'

'Where then?'

'Immediately we get clear of the Hall we look for Lady Garroway and her daughters.'

'Immediately?'

'The Prince insists.' Webb sounded annoyed.

'Very well,' Arne said and looked at Lorrimar. Lorrimar shrugged his shoulders.

'Let's get moving,' he said.

Outside the house Kurusu had opened his mouth to give the order to advance closer to the house when he saw a movement near the garage. A man moved across the front of the house and disappeared from sight behind the big car that stood on the gravelled forecourt. Kurusu waited and then slowly, so slowly at first that he thought his eyes were playing tricks in the darkness, the car began to move forward. He snapped at one of his men to move across the grass, ready to cut off the car if there was an attempt to bring it down the drive but then the car stopped. Suddenly the figure came into sight again and ran back towards the front of the house. Kurusu saw the door open and the man slipped inside. He felt a hand grip his arm and he turned his head and saw a tongue of flame inside the vehicle. His mind rapidly checked the probabilities. He told two of the men to stay where they were and he ran to join the man who was already closing in on the car. Together they ran in a wide circle, keeping well clear of the car that was already clearly silhouetted against the house by the flames that were filling the interior. They reached the back of the house and joined the two men already in position there. Then there was an explosion from the front of the house and he brought up his AK 47 and waited. There was no movement at any of the windows and the door stayed closed. At the same instant that he realised he had assumed the wrong probability he heard shots from the front of the Hall. He sprinted to the front, this time taking a direct route that took him close to the wall of the building. He paused as he came level with the front of the Hall. The Rolls-Royce was a mass of flame and burning fuel was spreading through the gravel. He glanced to his left and then to his right and ran swiftly across to where he had left the two men. He saw their bodies as he approached and moved straight on without stopping to see whether or not they were dead, but behind him one of the three men paused and checked the two bodies. At the bottom of the slope Kurusu waited for the others. Then the four men moved off towards the church where they had left their hostages.

Only a short distance ahead of the Japanese terrorists the group of men from the house had split into two. The leading party of the Prince, his bodyguard and Garroway had Lieutenant Webb guiding them. Martin had received a flesh wound in the exchange of fire as they had burst out of the house, but it was in his forearm and did not hamper his movements. The second group was moving more slowly. Lorrimar and Arne were half-carrying McKendrick. The little man had been hit in the chest and shoulder and was in great pain and kept losing consciousness. With Mannion, a less reluctant captive than he had been, keeping a few paces ahead of them they were almost a hundred yards behind when the leading party reached the path that led up to the church. Webb stopped and waited for the others to join him. He looked at McKendrick.

'How is he?' he asked.

'Not good,' Lorrimar said.

'We'd better . . .' Webb stopped speaking as Arne reached out and gripped her arm.

'Listen,' Arne said. There was silence for a moment.

'What did you hear?' Webb asked.

'I'm not sure but I think it came from the church.' Webb glanced up at the dark building.

'I didn't hear anything.'

'I'm not certain I did, but I think we should take a look.'

'Okay.'

'Do we split up?' Webb hesitated a moment before replying.

'No,' he said after a moment. 'We stay together.' He turned away and began to walk up the path towards the church. Just short of the building he stopped and waited and then with Martin close behind him he moved towards the main door. Lorrimar was trying to make McKendrick comfortable on the ground beside a well-kept gravestone when shots were fired from the church. He heard a screaming cry from one of the men outside the doorway, a cry that ended abruptly. Lorrimar swept up one of the AKM's and dived for cover behind the headstone of the grave where McKendrick lay. As he did so he was aware that Arne had flung himself towards where Garroway and the Prince were hidden amongst the gravestones. At the church door there was more firing. This time it was louder, either Webb or Martin were firing into the building. There was a cry from inside the church and, muffled though the sound was, Lorrimar was in no doubt that it was a woman's voice. Moments later he saw Webb run back towards him, crouched low.

'Did you hear that?' he said as he came up.

'Yes. They've got a woman in there.'

'Yes, by Christ, and I've hit her.'

'Not your fault. What happened to Martin?'

'Dead. He took a full burst in the chest.'

'Bloody hell.'

'Do you suppose the woman I hit was . . .' Webb hesitated unwilling to go on.

'If it was, all the more reason to get in there fast,' Lorrimar snapped. 'Come on, we'd better decide what we do next.' He crawled across to

236

Arne and the others with the young officer following him. 'Martin's dead,' he announced as he arrived. He looked at Garroway. 'There's a possibility your wife and daughters are in there,' he said. 'Did you hear...'

'I heard the scream,' Garroway said. 'Who fired?'

'I did,' Webb replied. Garroway looked at the soldier.

'If you did hit my wife or one of my daughters then I understand fully that the responsibility was not yours.' The financier turned and looked coldly at Lorrimar. 'That responsibility lies elsewhere.' Webb looked from Garroway to Lorrimar, an uncertain expression on his face. Neither man chose to explain to him. It was Arne who brought them back to their predicament.

'Right,' he said. 'We guessed wrong. We still need cover and we can't stay here. The men at the house will be following us down here now and we'll end up trapped between them and the men in the church.' He looked at Webb. 'Any idea how many are inside?'

'Definitely two,' Webb replied. 'Whether there are more than that I don't know, but I heard two weapons being fired.'

'I think we should move out of this graveyard,' Arne said. 'The nearest buildings are Home Farm which means going back down the lane to the main road or we can cut across to the cottages and the village shop. From there it's only a few yards to the inn and the radio in the Landrover.'

'I'm staying here,' Garroway said. The others looked at him. He pointed to the church. 'If my wife and my daughters are in there then I'm staying.'

'We can't risk splitting up,' Webb said. 'If we do that they'll pick us off easily.'

'I'm staying,' Garroway said flatly.

'No,' Webb said. 'My first duty has to be to protect the Prince. To do that I want all the firepower together in one place and that isn't going to be here.'

'Why not?' Garroway demanded. 'Taking refuge in another building doesn't improve the position we were in at the Hall. We are as well off in the open. At least we are less susceptible to attack by light artillery. If they have any.'

'He's right,' Lorimar said.

'I agree too,' a quiet voice interrupted. They all looked at the Prince. 'I understand your position Lieutenant,' he went on. 'However if I decide to stay here then you will have to stay here too. Is that not so?'

'Yes Sir,' Webb said uncertainly.

'Very well, I will stay here.' There was a moment's silence and then from a few yards away they heard a sound.

'Dave,' a weak voice called out. Lorimar crossed to where McKendrick lay.

'What is it mate?' he asked.

'Mannion. He's gone. Taken my Beretta. Down there.' The injured man pointed and Lorrimar turned and caught a fleeting glimpse of the fat man running towards the road. At that moment there was a sudden burst of firing and Lorrimar could hear bullets slapping into the trees along the path. Mannion stumbled and fell, calling out in a plaintive, yelping way as he did so.

'They've winged him,' McKendrick said.

'That's what friends are for,' Lorrimar said softly. Mannion scrambled to his knees and began to crawl along the path towards the gunman, calling out as he did so.

'It's me, Mannion. Don't shoot.' There was a long silence, broken suddenly by a single shot. Dirt kicked up off the path a few feet in front of the crawling man. He screamed thinly, not in pain but in fear. A second shot kicked up more dirt and Mannion turned and scrambled to his feet and began a lurching, stumbling run, back towards the church. He was half-way along the path when the firing began again, not single shots this time but a short, intense burst. The fat man was thrown forward to his knees, surprisingly no sound coming from him. Lorrimar began to move forward, but McKendrick gripped his arm, his fingers digging in with unexpected strength.

'No Dave. Leave the bastard. He deserves all

he gets.' Lorrimar hesitated, tense, and then Mannion reared to his feet again and at the same instant another longer burst of firing cut through the silence. Mannion's head seemed to dissolve into a spray of fine particles and his body, almost as if it had a life of its own, moved jerkily forward and then abruptly subsided, limp and drained, into a crumpled heap on the ground. Lorrimar looked down at McKendrick.

'Two down, two to go,' he said lightly.

'Yeah,' the little man said. 'And very likely it'll be three down soon.

'Don't talk like that mate,' Lorrimar said.

'Don't kid Dave. This is a bad one. Look, if I do flake out then don't let them tell me Mum will you. I expect she wouldn't understand anyway, but just to be on the safe side. Keep it from her. Okay?'

'If it comes to that okay but it won't.' Lorrimar tried to see the extent of McKendrick's wounds, but gave up when he cried out with the pain. Webb looked at Arne.

'When the other group get here we're in trouble.'

'What can we do?'

'Get into the church. That way we get the women back, eliminate at least two of the enemy and give ourselves more protective cover.'

'Unless we get everyone killed in the attempt.'

'I think it's a risk we have to take.' Webb

240

turned to the Prince. 'I think you should stay out of this Sir,' he said.

'No Lieutenant,' the Prince said softly, taking care that his voice did not carry. 'I am sorry to have to disagree with you again, but we are reduced in numbers. You need me to defend the position. And not with this.' He held up the ancient Ceska Lorrimar had given him earlier that night. Webb nodded.

'Yes sir,' he said. 'Take up a position over there. I'll reorganise the weapons to give us a better spread of fire.' He crawled over to Arne. 'See anything?'

'No.' Arne said. 'But it will be light soon. You can already see those trees more clearly. At least we're looking east. We should have them in silhouette before they see us. We'll have to pray that it's going to be a cloudy morning. We don't want the early morning sun striking into our faces.'

'What is the layout of the church?' Webb asked.

'Cruciform in shape. Main door at the front as you know. Two more doors, one in the north arm of the transept, one in the south, both doors facing the front of the church.'

'I see.'

'What are you planning?'

'How to get in without being killed in the process.' Arne looked at the young lieutenant. He started to speak and then changed his mind.

241

There didn't seem much point in saying something they all knew. They would have been in a no less dangerous position if they had stayed at the Hall.

CHAPTER TWENTY-SEVEN

Mason saw the movement beyond the barricade and cautiously moved to where he could see the figures of the two men. As he watched, one of the men moved quietly away from his position and headed towards the village. Mason slipped into the police car and called up the other cars and asked for any changes in their situation. One of the cars, the one on Stonor Road, had also noticed a man leave his position. Mason sat in the car and considered the reasons that could have made the men leave their posts. He came to the conclusion that they had been recalled either by radio or by pre-arrangement. In either case it meant that something was happening in the village. He checked his watch and wondered aloud what was keeping the Task Force and the army. Abruptly he reached a decision. He called up the other cars and waited until Jackson and Armstrong were listening.

'Leave one man in position, then move into the village. Try to avoid trouble with the men on the barriers.' He paused, realising that he had already said enough to give away their intention if the other side was listening on the radio frequency. 'I'll pick up the two extra men,' he went on, deciding that it was too late to worry about being overheard. He climbed out of the car and crossed to one of the two men with him. 'Find the two men in the lane. They should be about half a mile down from the corner. Tell them to move in towards the big house. You come back here and stay here, keep an eye on their last man. If he leaves his post follow him. And watch yourself.' With the second man Mason climbed across the ditch and began to follow the path the young soldier had followed. He was still well short of the village when he began to regret the passing of the years. He was tired and cold. Then he heard the explosion from the direction of the Hall, followed by several bursts of firing and suddenly the tiredness left him. He stopped and considered what Manning had told him. He decided that the firing from the house had been either an assault from the attackers or some sort of defence. He was undecided where to head and then concluded that as far as he knew the house was where the Prince and the Garroways were being held and that was where he had to be. He turned off to his right and moved on, facing into the sky that was beginning to lighten. He had reached the road when he saw a movement. He stopped and waited, and after a few moments he saw the movement had been made by four men. All uniformed and all armed. Mason hesitated and then decided to continue on towards the house. He was almost up to the Hall and could clearly see the wreckage of a car smouldering in front of the building when the two men who had been despatched up through the woods came into view. Mason walked to meet them.

'Nobody in the house sir,' one of them reported. 'There's two men dead just up there.'

'Right,' Mason said. 'There's a house over there, servants' cottage from what Klein told us. We'd better take a look there.' The four policemen had reached the cottage when they heard the firing from the north. Mason turned. 'You,' he snapped at one of the men. 'Check the cottage. The rest of you come with me.' He started off down the drive towards the road, cursing to himself for deciding to check the Hall first. As far as he could tell the firing had come from near the church and he would have been there if he hadn't changed direction. He broke into a run and the other men followed. Ahead he heard more shooting. 'Where the bloody hell is the army?' he muttered to himself as he ran.

CHAPTER TWENTY-EIGHT

A hail of bullets smashed into the grey stonework of the church high above the doorway. Webb glanced up from where he lay with the others.

'High,' he said. 'Too high for just bad shooting. They're trying to tell us something.'

'They're telling us to keep our bloody heads down,' Lorrimar said.

'Maybe. I'm not sure.' There was a heavy, rolling report from the direction of the terrorists' position. Moments later there was an explosion from about forty yards south of the church. Mud and stones pattered down.

'What was that?'

'Grenade of some kind I think. They must have a grenade-launcher out there. Or a mortar. That's what they're telling us. They have the range of the church and they have the means of blowing it apart.'

'Then . . .'

'They're telling us we give up or they'll open fire on the church.'

'Their own men are inside.'

'I don't think that will bother Kurusu.'

'So what do we do?'

'Two things. We counter-attack, but before that we get the hostages out of the church.'

Webb slipped away and ran round to where Arne was covering the door in the northern arm of the transept. 'We're going in,' he said. 'I'll send Garroway here with you, Lorrimar can go in through the other transept door. I'll take the main door.'

'What about the Prince?' Arne asked. Webb hesitated.

'I don't want him involved, but I expect he'll overrule me again. If he does I'll let him come in with you and put Garroway with Lorrimar.'

'No.' Arne said. 'We don't know what we're going to find in there. Keep Lorrimar and Garroway apart until we do. I'll have Garroway here and let the Prince go in with Lorrimar if you can't talk him into staying out of sight.'

'Why is Garroway at odds with Lorrimar? What's been going on here?'

'It will take too long Lieutenant. I'll explain later.' Webb nodded his head.

'Okay,' he said. 'I'll send Garroway round. You'll hear me go in. Give me a few seconds' start then you come in. We don't know where they'll be and it's going to be dark in there so we'll all have to be alert and quick. Try to stay within the walls of the transept. I'll tell the others to do the same.'

'Where will you be?'

'Tell me about the interior. What will I find when I go in?'

'Across the entrance is a glass and timber

screen. It serves as a draught excluder. You can see through it and that means you can be seen as well. You may very well have smashed the glass when you fired into the church earlier. The pews are arranged in two banks with a wide centre aisle and two narrower ways down either wall.'

'Okay, unless something happens when I get inside that makes me change my mind, I'll go to my right which will bring me to the side aisle on this side of the building. So try to avoid firing over here if you can.'

'You'll be in more danger from a stray shot from Lorrimar and the Prince than from us.'

'Yes, I'll tell them to be careful. Right, give me a couple of minutes to explain what we're doing to the others and for Garroway to get here. Then stand by.'

'I'll be ready. Take care Lieutenant.'

It took the lieutenant longer than he had expected to set up the assault on the church and by the time everyone was in position he was casting anxious glances towards the road, half-expecting the main body of terrorists to lose patience and begin an attack. Despite not knowing what awaited them inside the church, it was with a feeling that amounted to almost relief that he finally gave the command and launched himself at the heavy doors that opened into the church. As he burst through into the building he threw himself down, using his impetus to carry him forward towards the screen Arne had described. He heard a burst of firing and a spray of bullets splattered against the walls only a few feet over where he lay. He scrambled forward and moved to his left until he could feel the screen with his right hand. Then silently he reversed his movement and went away to his right, the unfamiliar AK 47 he had taken from the man he had killed in the field gripped firmly in his hands.

Arne and Garroway had used the few moments they had before entering the building to hastily improvise their intended movements. As they went in through the doorway Garroway dropped to the floor and crawled to his left, his eyes searching into the darkness for some sign of his family. Arne moved straight to the back wall of the transept and, remaining upright, he covered the other man's position.

Lorrimar and the Prince both stayed close to the floor of the church with the younger man positioning himself in much the same way as Garroway had done at the opposite side of the building while Lorrimar went past him, almost as far as the centre aisle. Unlike the others Lorrimar kept most of his attention towards the altar. Webb had suggested the possibility, however slight, that the men inside the church had moved into that area in order to make a stand from there.

The shots fired at Webb served to locate the

terrorists' position. They were mid-way along the southern wall of the main body of the building. In the flash of light Arne saw the two men for just a fleeting instant, but that barest glimpse was enough to reveal that the women were not in sight. Unhesitatingly he opened fire with the AKM. He got off three shots before he ran for a new position close to Lorrimar, but at the opposite side of the centre aisle.

'Did you see them?' Arne asked.

'Yes, but I didn't see anyone else.'

'Neither did...' From the front of the church there was another short burst of gunfire from Webb and as the echo died they could hear a low moaning coming from the area where they had seen the two men.

'He's got one I think,' Lorrimar said. He started to move down the centre aisle and then, clearly in the silence they all heard Sarah Garroway's voice.

'You've hit them both.' Lorrimar stood up and ran across between two pews and down the side aisle. The two men were lying against the wall. In the greyish light that was starting to come in through the high windows Lorrimar could see that both were dead. He turned to look for Sarah Garroway. He found her between two pews, she was kneeling down, her mother's head cradled in her lap. There was a dark stain across Lady Garroway's dress. Lorrimar instinctively looked up to locate Sir James.

Then as the others began to gather around he heard shots from outside the building.

'Bill,' he said and ran down the side aisle towards the main door. He heard someone following him as he reached the doorway and he ran recklessly into the cold grey light of the morning. He reached the place where they had left McKendrick and stopped. Behind him Lieutenant Webb gripped his shoulder and pulled him down to the ground.

'Keep down,' Webb said.

'Where is he?' Lorrimar asked.

'There,' Webb pointed. Lorrimar looked along Webb's arm. McKendrick was stumbling along the path away from the church. He was swaying from side to side as he half-ran, half-walked.

'Bill,' Lorrimar yelled, but the little man kept on moving. Lorrimar and Webb stared helplessly and then there were two shots from the trees by the road and McKendrick staggered and fell. Then, miraculously, he scrambled to his knees and raised one arm. He swung his entire body behind his arm and something flew out of his hand and curved into the trees.

'Grenade,' Lorrimar said. 'Come on let's go.' He was on his feet and running, weaving in between gravestones, before Webb reacted. As he came to his feet to follow the other man he heard the grenade explode and saw a flash of orange light. He caught up with Lorrimar just as firing started up again in the trees. Bullets smacked into the headstones around them and the two men flung themselves to the ground.

'We'd better get back to the church. We can't reach him and the chances are he's already dead,' Webb said.

'Why did he do it?' Lorrimar said softly. 'He never stood a chance.'

'The wound was bad. Maybe he thought he would die anyway and that there was a better way than just lying here.'

'Christ,' Lorrimar said, 'he didn't have to do it like John Wayne.'

'Come on,' Webb said and began to back away between the graves. After a moment Lorrimar followed. Behind them they heard one or two shots and the hiss of bullets passing through the air over their heads. Then there was silence. They reached the church and went inside. Arne came towards them as they came in past the shattered glass screen.

'What happened?' he asked and Webb told him briefly. Arne glanced at Lorrimar. 'Sorry,' he said. Lorrimar shrugged.

'Three down and one to go,' he said. Arne looked at him carefully for a moment.

'Lady Garroway is badly injured,' he said. Lorrimar glanced fleetingly at the small, silent group against the wall, then he looked back to Arne.

'Us or them?' he asked.

'According to Sarah it happened earlier.' He looked at Webb. 'It must have been when you . . .' his voice trailed off. Webb started to move towards the others.

'I'd better . . .'

'No.' Arne caught his arm. 'Not now. Wait. We'd better prepare for the attack.' Webb hesitated and then nodded his head.

'Yes,' he said. 'They must do something now. Either break off or make a final attack. They must know that we're bound to be reinforced soon.'

'What can they do?' Lorrimar asked.

'Destroy the church and us in it.'

'It still leaves them without any gain. They set out to kidnap the Prince. What do they gain by killing him?'

'They gain what a lot of groups like them have been gaining from killing innocent people all over the world,' Webb said. 'Nothing. At least nothing that you or I or any of us would understand.'

'I still can't see . . .' Lorrimar began when an explosion rocked the buildings. Small pieces of masonry rattled down onto the floor and the pews.

'Get everyone up to the altar,' Webb snapped. 'Use whatever is movable to provide shelter from falling stonework or shrapnel. That was high on the wall. If one comes in through a window we're in trouble.' Hastily they

252

shepherded everyone to the west end of the church then, leaving Garroway with his daughters, Webb drew the others a short distance away.

'I don't like sitting here waiting,' he said. As he spoke a second explosion shook the building. 'I think they've moved away to the north to get that angle for their firing. There can't be many of them left. I think we should try to get a party out of the door in the south transept and they can make a wide, circular move and try to get behind their position.'

'I'll go,' Arne said. 'I know my way around here.'

'Agreed, it will be you and me,' Webb said.

'You, sir, and you,' he said to the Prince and Lorrimar. 'Stay here, keep close to the others and don't come outside unless they really get your range and start dropping things inside.' He turned before either man could voice a protest and led Arne away to the door. Moments later the two men had disappeared from sight. Lorrimar looked at the young man and for a moment the absurdity of his position registered in his mind and he grinned slightly.

'Tell me,' the young man said. 'Did you know I would be there, at the Hall, when you made your plans?'

'No. We weren't idiots. At least not that kind of idiot. Mind you we must have been nuts to fall for Mannion's double-game.'

'Why did he need to make such a complicated plan? Why didn't this man Kurusu simply make a direct attempt to take me prisoner? It shouldn't have been too difficult.'

'No I suppose not. One detective sergeant isn't the best defence in the world.'

'It's all we have needed in the past.'

'It isn't the past now,' Lorrimar said.

'No it isn't. Why didn't he make a direct attempt? Why involve you?'

'I've no idea. Except that it would be easier, less likely to attract attention if we were seen floating about than if they had made their own preliminary arrangements. It also meant that if something went wrong at the very beginning they could fade away and try again. Nobody would have thought *we* were trying to get at you.'

'Perhaps not. However, it seems that things did go the wrong way from the start.'

'You can say that again,' said Lorrimar. Above them glass shattered and the two men dived for cover. The crash of sound as the grenade exploded on the floor of the church temporarily deafened Lorrimar and then as his head cleared he saw that no one had been hurt. The grenade had landed among the pews to the right of the centre aisle and a twisted pile of timber stuck grotesquely into the air. From outside he heard sporadic shooting. Then he glanced again at the Garroways. They were all

254

looking past him to the door in the south wing of the transept. He started to turn when he heard the quiet, familiar voice.

'Stand perfectly still Mr. Lorrimar. Any unnecessary movement should be avoided.' Lorrimar made himself relax. He stood there, facing the altar, the Prince a pace in front of him. Behind him he heard footsteps approaching and he steeled himself for the expected bullet.

CHAPTER TWENTY-NINE

When the grenade exploded in the trees where the church path led off the road, Mason stopped and, with his men, took cover by the roadside. He heard more shots and shook his head slightly.

'Let's go carefully lads,' he said. 'I don't know who's firing at who, so for heaven's sake make certain you know who you're aiming at before you press the trigger.' He started forward again and at that moment he heard shots from some distance away. He looked in the direction of the sound. 'Thank God for that,' he said. 'The Task Force have arrived. Them or the army or with luck, both.'

'Do we wait sir?' One of the men with him asked. Mason shook his head.

255

'No, better not take the chance. Let's find out what's happening at the church.'

The four policemen moved carefully into the trees that bordered the graveyard. They found one dead man where the explosion had occurred. There wasn't a lot of him left but what there was was still covered in pieces of uniform. They moved on through the trees and entered the graveyard, spreading out to cover the full width of the ground.

'Over here sir,' the man nearest to the path called out softly. Mason crossed to where the man was crouched over a body.

'Christ, it's Bill McKendrick,' Mason said.

'There's another one over there,' the sergeant said. 'It's that soldier. Manning. His throat's been cut.'

'Bloody hell,' Mason said. He hesitated for a moment and then straightened up. 'Come on,' he said. He moved slowly along the path and then stopped when he saw another body. He looked down and then glanced at the sergeant. 'Another one,' he said. 'God, this is going to take some unravelling.' He hesitated for a moment. 'We'd better get a move on,' he said. 'At this rate the men with the Prince are likely to be outnumbered.' He set off down the path at a brisker pace and after only the slightest pause the sergeant followed. From among the gravestones the other policemen saw the Chief Superintendent quicken his pace and they moved across the churchyard and fell in behind him.

Arne and Webb found the position of the grenade-launcher without difficulty. They had moved around the western end of the church after leaving by the door in the southern wing of the transept. They heard the explosions as more grenades were fired at the church.

'That last one went inside,' Webb said grimly.

'There he is,' Arne said. 'He's in that small clump of trees. There, to the right of the telegraph pole.'

'I've got him.' Webb thought for a moment. 'We'll split up, you take the left flank and I'll take . . .'

'Wait,' Arne said.

'What is it?'

'Men coming up the path.'

'Christ, more of them.'

'No, I don't think so. They're not in uniform.'

'Well they're asking for it if they keep coming. They're in clear view of us and the men with the grenade-launcher.' At that moment there was a burst of automatic rifle fire from the clump of trees and the four men on the path scattered as they dived for cover.

'Well,' Arne said. 'At least that tells us they're on our side, whoever they are.'

'Right. We'd better put that emplacement out

of action. We'll both take the left flank. That way we won't get between the position and the men on the pathway. If they make a break for it that way, we'll have to hope the new arrivals are good shots.' He led the way towards the left and gradually moved into a position where they had reasonable cover between them and the grenade-launcher. Webb looked at Arne.

'Ready?' he asked.

'When you are.' Webb nodded and eased up into a crouch.

'Right,' he said. 'I'll move in twenty five yards. Give me covering fire. Then you follow.' He ran forward in a low crouch and Arne set up a steady covering fire into the trees ahead of the young lieutenant. When he saw Webb stop he held his fire and tensed and then as Webb waved him on he ran towards the new position. Webb began a sustained burst of covering fire and stopped as Arne dropped to the ground beside him.

'I don't like it,' Webb said.

'What?'

'No return fire and no more grenades launched towards the church.'

'You're not thinking we've been drawn away from another attacking position?'

'Could be. Let's get in there fast and see what we're facing. Ready?'

'Yes.' Webb ran on again, another twenty five yards, with Arne providing covering fire. Then

Arne moved up and joined him.

'One more and we're there.' Webb started forward. He had gone less than half the remaining distance when there were three shots from the trees. Arne saw the movement of branches and re-directed his fire. He emptied the AKM and then looked for Webb. He could just make out the lieutenant's body lying in long grass a few yards short of the trees. Arne hesitated and then hastily re-loaded the rifle. He fired another burst into the trees and ran on. He passed the soldier's body and crashed into the trees. There was one man there. He was lying slumped against a tree, one arm draped against the grenade-launcher. He was dead. Arne quickly checked around him. There was no one else there. He ran to where Webb lay. The three shots he had heard had all found their target. The front of Webb's jacket was stained with blood and there was a bigger stain spreading on the ground beneath his body. His eyes were open. Arne heard someone approaching and spun round, bringing the AKM up into position. He saw four men, all in ordinary clothes.

'Who are you?' he called out.

'Police.' Arne turned away and laid down the rifle. Webb looked up at him.

'Like Lorrimar said, better than the U.S. Cavalry.' He closed his eyes. After a moment Arne reached for the rifle and stood up. He looked at the oldest of the four men.

'Do you know what's going on here?' he asked.

'We know enough,' the man said.

'The Prince is in the church and there are very probably two or three more terrorists around.'

'We'd better get moving then,' Mason said. The five men started to run towards the church.

CHAPTER THIRTY

Kurusu walked round Lorrimar and the Prince and then, after glancing at Garroway and his daughters, he casually turned his back on them and looked carefully at the Prince.

'Please lay down any weapons you have,' he said quietly. After the briefest hesitation the young man did as he had been commanded.

'Now you Mr. Lorrimar,' Kurusu said. Lorrimar hesitated for several long moments and then he saw the terrorist's eyes flicker slightly and he heard a light step behind him. He slowly drew one of the .44 Smith & Wessons from his pocket and laid it and the rifle he carried on the stone floor of the church. The footsteps behind him stopped. 'Is that everything Mr. Lorrimar?' Kurusu asked. Lorrimar hesitated again and then shook his head. He brought out the second .44 and added that to the other weapons. 'Good,' Kurusu said. He jerked his head slightly and the second man came past Lorrimar and the Prince and pushed the guns away with his foot. He walked past Kurusu and went up to Sir James Garroway. Lorrimar watched as the man took the rifle from the financier and then walked back to stand beside his taller companion. 'Good,' Kurusu said again. 'Now we are going, just we four,' his gesture included Lorrimar and the Prince. 'But before we do I have something to show you Sir James.' He turned and pulled open his jacket. Lorrimar saw Garroway's eyes widen slightly and then Kurusu turned back and Lorrimar saw that across his chest, hanging from a harness over his shoulder, was a block of grey material that looked almost like modelling clay. 'Plastic explosive,' Kurusu said. He turned back to Garroway. 'You will warn anyone who intends following us of this,' he said. 'Please assure them that in the event of an attack I shall detonate the explosive and everyone with me will die.' He looked speculatively at Garroway. 'I very much hope that you believe me Sir James and that you can convince the others. If you do not . . .' He shrugged his shoulders and turned back to Lorrimar and the Prince. 'Enough time has been wasted.' He raised the automatic weapon he held. 'Go,' he said. The four men walked out of the church with Kurusu keeping close to the two Englishmen. The second terrorist was several paces ahead until Kurusu called to him and spoke quickly in his own language. Then the man fell back and the four, now in a tight-knit group, crossed the churchyard to the wall that bounded the field where the helicopters lay.

'Your helicopters are out of action,' Lorrimar said. Kurusu looked at him. 'I'm not kidding,' Lorrimar went on. 'Webb put them out earlier. You won't get out that way.' Kurusu hesitated for a moment.

'Then we'll go out by car,' he said. Lorrimar shrugged. Kurusu's apparent calm acceptance concealed the fact that he was savagely angry with the way things had completely left his control. Letting the men he had previously had pinned down in the Hall get between him and his hostages had been bad enough. When it was obvious that the two guards he had left at the church had been killed or captured and the hostages freed he had sunk into a cold silence, aware that the remaining men under his command were beginning to doubt his ability. He had ordered the attack with the grenade-launcher in a fit of rage and then he had realised that by moving the site of the launcher to a position where the men in the church could reach it, he stood a chance of splitting the group. It had worked and he finally had the Prince. He hastily considered the loss of the helicopters. He did not doubt that Lorrimar had spoken the truth. He mentally abandoned the men remaining at the barricades. He decided that he would let Lorrimar live to drive the car, leaving himself and his colleague to fire on anyone who attempted to take the Prince away from them. The loss of the three men did not disturb him. Every cause needed its martyrs.

They climbed over the wall and in the field their pace quickened and they soon reached the roadway. Still close together they crossed the road and entered the driveway that led up to Fenton Hall. When they reached Sarah Garroway's Porsche, Kurusu stopped.

'A little small for four of us, but it will serve,' he said.

'My car's at the Hall,' Lorrimar said quickly.

'Yes, of course,' Kurusu said. 'We will take it.' The four men moved up the drive. It was almost fully light and Lorrimar scanned the area as he walked, desperately trying to find some way of distracting the two gunmen. They reached the gravelled forecourt and passed the still-smoking wreckage of the Rolls Royce. In front of the garage they stopped.

'Open the door,' Kurusu ordered. Lorrimar tried the door handle.

'It's locked,' he said. 'I forgot, the keys are inside.' Kurusu looked at him, his eyes blazing angrily.

'No tricks Lorrimar,' he said softly.

263

'No, I forgot. They're inside.'

'Get them,' Kurusu said and added something to the other man in Japanese. Lorrimar walked to the front door of the Hall and went in with the second terrorist close behind him. Lorrimar walked through to the kitchen and picked up the keys from the table. As he did so he glanced up and saw a figure running across the lawn at the back of the house. The man was dressed exactly as the other terrorists and although the light was behind him Lorrimar was certain he was Japanese. At that same instant the man with him saw the running man and a wide grin appeared on his face and he started towards the door that led from the kitchen to the garden. Lorrimar glanced sideways and saw a rack of kitchen knives. Unhesitatingly he reached out and pulled a short-bladed knife from the rack. The man heard the sound and started to turn, but Lorrimar had already closed the gap between them and he buried the knife in the man's body, his other hand covering the wide-open mouth to prevent any sound escaping. He carefully lowered the body to the floor and stood up. There was no sign of the man he had seen from the window. He picked up the automatic rifle the dead man had carried and then reached into his pocket and pulled out the hand grenade he had been carrying for most of the night. He looked at it.

'Good for you Jim,' he said softly. He eased open the door and went out of the house. Behind the garage was the fuel oil tank that supplied the central heating boiler for the house. Lorrimar tried the window in the back wall of the garage. He eased it open and then turned away and clambered up onto the tank and then onto the roof. He moved forward until he could hear Kurusu's voice. He looked over the edge of the roof and saw the tall Japanese talking rapidly to the other man who had appeared. Lorrimar craned his neck and he saw several figures spreading over the lower part of the lawn. Most of them were uniformed and they were making no attempt to close in on the house. He glanced down again and at that instant the Prince looked up and saw him. The young man's expression did not change and Lorrimar gently motioned with his head. He tried to indicate that he wanted the Prince to move slightly to the right. He did so and Lorrimar eased backwards and dropped from the roof onto the fuel tank and then to the ground. He opened the window and climbed through into the garage. The Daimler was facing forward and he opened the car door carefully, slipped into the driving seat and put the key in the ignition. At that moment he heard Kurusu call out in Japanese. Then after a short pause he called again.

'Lorrimar.' Lorrimar took a deep breath and

turned the ignition key. The engine roared into life and he released the handbrake and pushed the selector lever into drive all in one fluid motion. The car leaped forward and smashed through the door. In a confused split-second of time Lorrimar saw that the Prince was already moving well to the right and Kurusu, his face twisted in anger, was starting to follow. The bonnet of the Daimler struck the terrorist and he was thrown up into the air to land, sprawled up against the windscreen. Over the sound of the engine Lorrimar heard shots and he risked a glance in the rear-view mirror. He saw the last terrorist lying on the ground and the Prince still standing. Then he looked at Kurusu. One of his hands was gripping a windscreen wiper and the other was fumbling inside his jacket. Lorrimar kept his foot hard on the accelerator and the car rocked and bounced as it gathered speed down the long, sloping lawn. He pulled the hand grenade from his pocket and raised it to his mouth. He pulled the safety pin out with his teeth.

'Now I'm doing it like John Wayne,' he muttered. He dropped the grenade on the floor of the car, opened the door and threw himself out onto the grass. As he rolled over on the hard wet ground he felt a snapping pain in his shoulder. Behind him the car sped on down the slope with Kurusu still clinging to it. Then suddenly the car exploded with a shattering roar. Parts of it went on rolling down the slope and blazing petrol spilled over the grass. As Lorrimar watched, the main chassis and body stopped moving. He saw Kurusu plainly, the man was still alive and looking towards where he lay. Then the terrorist's hands moved and there was a second explosion, this time bigger than the first. There was flame and smoke and pieces of something were thrown up into the air. When the smoke cleared there was even less of the car left. There was no sign of the man.

Lorrimar stood up unsteadily and watched as the soldiers moved up the slope towards him. Among them were a number of men in civilian clothes. He recognised two of them. He grinned at Arne as he came up.

'Okay?' he asked.

'Yes. You?'

'Yes. How's Webb?'

'He'll live.' Lorrimar nodded at Arne. The two men looked at one another. After a moment Arne grinned slightly.

'Well done,' he said. Lorrimar turned to the other man.

'Hello Mr. Mason, I thought you wouldn't be far away.'

'Hello Dave. This is a bigger mess than you usually leave for us to clear up.' Mason glanced away and Lorrimar followed his look. The Prince was walking down the lawn towards them. The young man stopped and smiled at

Lorrimar.

'How are you?' he asked.

'I'll survive,' Lorrimar said. The Prince nodded his head.

'Thank you,' he said. He looked down towards the road. A police car was negotiating the Porsche. Inside it were Sarah Garroway and her sister. The Prince started to walk towards the car. The three men stood watching him. From the road the alarm bell of an ambulance rang out.

'That will be Webb and Lady Garroway,' Arne said.

'So they all live happily ever after,' Lorrimar said. He looked at Mason. 'I think you'd better take me to hospital,' he said. Mason raised his eyebrows. 'I think I've broken something in my shoulder,' Lorrimar said.

'Okay,' Mason said. 'While they're patching you up I'll try to work out what to charge you with first. With any amount of luck I'll get you put away for a hundred years.' Lorrimar looked across to where the tall figure of the Prince was leaning down over the police car talking to Sarah Garroway.

'Don't get too excited,' Lorrimar said. 'I think I've got a friend at court.'

Photoset, printed and bound in Great Britain by REDWOOD BURN LIMITED, Trowbridge, Wiltshire